BBC

DOCTOR WHO

THE TIME-TRAVELLING
ALMANAC

DOCTOR WHO

THE TIME-TRAVELLING
ALMANAC

THE OFFICIAL GUIDE
TO THE DOCTOR'S YEAR

SIMON GUERRIER

BBC
BOOKS

BBC Books, an imprint of Ebury Publishing
Penguin Random House UK
One Embassy Gardens, 8 Viaduct Gdns,
Nine Elms, London SW11 7BW

BBC Books is part of the Penguin Random House group of companies
whose addresses can be found at global.penguinrandomhouse.com

Penguin
Random House
UK

Doctor Who is produced in Wales by Bad Wolf with BBC Studios Productions

Executive Producers: Russell T Davies, Julie Gardner, Jane Tranter, Joel Collins & Phil Collinson

First published by BBC Books in 2024

www.penguin.co.uk

A CIP catalogue record for this book is available from the British Library

ISBN 9781785949173

Publishing Director: Albert DePetrillo
Project Editor: Steve Cole
Cover: Toby Clarke
Text Design: Jonathan Baker
Production: Antony Heller

Printed and bound in Great Britain by Clays Ltd, Elcograf S.p.A.

The authorised representative in the EEA is Penguin Random House Ireland,
Morrison Chambers, 32 Nassau Street, Dublin D02 YH68.

Penguin Random House is committed to a sustainable future for our business, our readers
and our planet. This book is made from Forest Stewardship Council® certified paper.

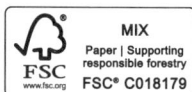

MIX
Paper | Supporting
responsible forestry
FSC® C018179

CONTENTS

INTRODUCTION **1**

JANUARY **6**

FEBRUARY **30**

MARCH **46**

APRIL **60**

MAY **80**

JUNE **100**

JULY **116**

AUGUST **134**

SEPTEMBER **154**

OCTOBER **172**

NOVEMBER **192**

DECEMBER **220**

ACKNOWLEDGEMENTS **249**

INTRODUCTION

DOCTOR
Wait, what year are you from?

RUBY
2024.

DOCTOR
Ooh, ha ha! Yikes... Spoilers!
Forget I said anything.

73 Yards by Russell T Davies (2024)

The Doctor won't tell Ruby Sunday exactly what the future holds. That involves spoilers and cheating.

Even so, if we want to be ready for what's coming, it helps to know what's been, and how the past and future are all connected to right now. Get a sense of your true position, your trajectory through time and space, and you'll be more alert to all the wonders going on.

The Doctor once told his friend Rose Tyler that our 'entire planet is hurtling round the Sun at 67,000 miles an hour'. That's an amazing 107,826 km per hour, or 18.5 miles / 29.8 km per second. That is *fast*, and yet most of the time we don't even notice.

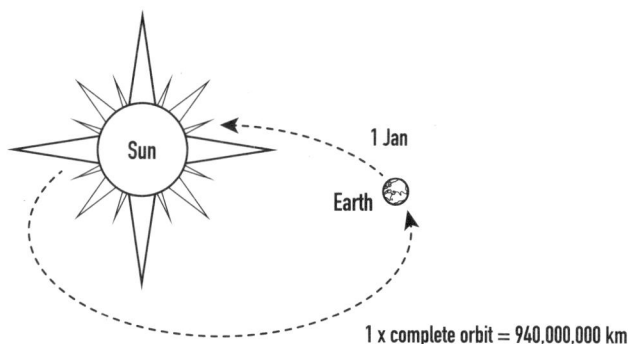

1 x complete orbit = 940,000,000 km

Even then, it takes 365.25 days to cover the 940 million km to complete an orbit around the Sun and come back to where we started. (It's not *exactly* where we started because the Sun is also moving through space.)

But think of it this way. Each day of the year is a point in that orbit. Right now, as you read this, you're in the same bit of the orbit as this time a year ago, and the year before that, stretching back into time.

And as we orbit, we're connected to that past. Each 1 January reminds us of the ones before. Every birthday, anniversary or mention of a past date connects us back in time, while we're moving ever onwards through time.

Because we're also heading forwards, moving at 1 second per second into the future.

The Earth keeps moving. We never stop on any date; we're always passing through. A new year or anniversary reminds us that we're *all* travellers in space and time.

Ruby Sunday gains this perspective by travelling in time and space with the Doctor. We hope to provide you with something similar in this book.

But what is an 'almanac' exactly? Well, to be honest, no one's really sure where the word comes from or its original meaning. The earliest known use of the word is from the year 1267, when monk, wizard and genius proto-scientist Roger Bacon used it to mean a collection of charts and other stuff detailing the movements of the Moon and objects in the sky. Bacon – who was also known as Doctor Mirabilis (meaning 'Doctor Amazing') – seems to have used this information as his own special guide through the year. Since then, popular almanacs have also included advice and observations, insights into history and science, recipes and jokes.

With that in mind, we've packed this book full of useful information and fun stuff to help enliven and illuminate your journey through 2025. Along the way, we'll provide ways to orient yourself in the universe, using the stars and your senses to get your bearings. We'll look at why Easter is on a different date every year, show you how to cook up a feast like Sylvia Noble and how the history of The Beatles is interwoven with that of the Doctor.

But we want you to take an active part in this book, too. Roger Bacon compiled his almanac because he didn't just accept what he read in other books, or what people in authority told him. He always wanted to test what was said.

So, with this book, we hope that you'll test it, play with it and see where it takes you. Most of all, we hope that whatever might be coming along in 2025, you have a great adventure.

Happy times and places
Simon

KEY

The information in this book is organised as follows:

♥♥ + ✈	Aircraft
♥♥ + 🎂	Birthday of actor with major role in *Doctor Who* or a character
♥♥ + 🎄	Christmas
♥♥ + ∩	Clothes
♥♥ + 🗼	Daleks
♥♥ + 🪩	Dancing
♥♥ + 📅	Dates in history
♥♥ + 🥚	Easter
♥♥ + 🏢	Empire State Building
♥♥ + 🚪	Exits from *Doctor Who*
♥♥ + 📺	First broadcast of an episode

* Episodes usually first broadcast in the UK – but when not we'll note their first broadcast *and* their first UK broadcast

♥♥ + 1st	First instance of something in *Doctor Who*
♥♥ + 🍽	Food and recipes
♥♥ + 🐨	Ha ha ha *ha* ha ha ha!
♥♥ + 🎵	Music
♥♥ + 🧭	Navigation

 Shark

❤❤ + 💬 Speech

❤❤ + 🪀 Spin-off TV series from *Doctor Who*

* All episodes are available to view for free on BBC iPlayer at time of writing but note that *Torchwood* and *Class* are aimed at an adult audience and contain adult themes, violence and upsetting scenes

❤❤ + 🚤 Submarine

❤❤ + 〰️ Tides

❤❤ + 🐝 Wasp

Space ❤❤ + ● New Moon

 Full Moon

❤❤ + ◑ Moon First Quarter

❤❤ + ◐ Moon Third Quarter

 Mars

 Mercury

 Neptune

 Saturn

 Venus

 Meteors

 Stars

 Sun

 Uranus

♥♥+
JANUARY

The TARDIS briefly stops in Trafalgar Square, London, as people celebrate New Year. This was surely meant to suggest that events on screen were happening on the same day as broadcast, the first (but not last) time this happens in *Doctor Who*.

But the episode was recorded on 3 December 1965 and used stock footage of Trafalgar Square, so it showed a New Year from at least 12 months before.

Where on Earth is Trafalgar Square?

Trafalgar Square in London appears in several *Doctor Who* stories. It's conquered by Daleks in *The Dalek Invasion of Earth* (1964); it's where Rose Tyler and her boyfriend Mickey Smith have lunch in *Rose* (2005). In *The Day of the Doctor* (2013), the Eleventh Doctor arrives in Trafalgar Square, hanging from the bottom of the TARDIS, which is in turn suspended from a helicopter.

Imagine trying to set the controls of the TARDIS to land in Trafalgar Square. How do we pinpoint a location on Earth?

For hundreds of years, we've mapped the Earth using a coordinate system based on the points of a compass.

To measure any position north to south, we use **latitude**. The northernmost point on Earth, the North Pole, is measured as 90° N. The Equator, straddling the middle of the Earth, is 0°. The southernmost point on Earth, the South Pole, is 90° S.

To measure any position east or west, we use **longitude** based on a starting point called the **prime meridian**. A meridian is an imaginary, straight line from the North Pole to the South Pole. We could measure from any such line, but since the 1890s the agreement has been to use the line that bisects Greenwich in London. This is measured as 0° longitude.

We then measure degrees either east or west of this prime meridian. The meridian directly opposite Greenwich on the other side of the world is both 180° E and 180° W. So, if you're setting the controls of the TARDIS:

- Trafalgar Square in London is 51.5080° N, 0.1281° W.
- Abbey Road Studios is relatively nearby at 51.5322° N, 0.1778° W; the Doctor and Ruby first meet The Beatles there (when it was called EMI Recording Studios).
- The Empire State Building in New York, where the First Doctor and the Tenth Doctor both encountered Daleks, is further away at 40.7484° N, 73.9857° W.
- Sydney Opera House in Australia, where the Twelfth Doctor takes Bill Potts, is 33.8568° S, 151.2153° E.

Empire State Building   Trafalgar Square
Abbey Road Studios

Sydney Opera House

01 JAN 1972 *Day of the Daleks* 1

01 JAN 1977 *The Face of Evil* 1

First appearance of warrior Leela of the Sevateem, who travels with the Fourth Doctor

01 JAN 2000 The Eighth Doctor kisses Dr Grace Holloway then heads off in the TARDIS.

01 JAN 2005 The dying Tenth Doctor speaks to Rose Tyler a few minutes into the new year and a few months before she meets his earlier self for the first time, in *The End of Time* 2 (2010).

01 JAN 2007 *The Sarah Jane Adventures: Invasion of the Bane* and *Torchwood: Captain Jack Harkness* and *End of Days*

First episode of spin-off series *The Sarah Jane Adventures*, which ran for 53 episodes

01 JAN 2010 *The End of Time* 2

First appearance of the Eleventh Doctor

01 JAN 2019 *Resolution*

A discovery at an archaeological site in Sheffield is bad news for the Doctor, with events taking place on the same day as broadcast.

01 JAN 2020 *Spyfall* 1

First appearance of a new incarnation of the Master

01 JAN 2021 *Revolution of the Daleks*

Ryan Sinclair and Graham O'Brien leave the TARDIS.

01 JAN 2022 *Eve of the Daleks*

Events seem to take place on the same day as broadcast but it's not stated on screen.

01 JAN 2025 Quadrantids

At the beginning of *Spearhead from Space* (1970), a UNIT radar station detects an incoming shower of meteors. The odd thing is that they're flying in formation – and heading for Oxley Woods in the UK, exactly the same spot on the ground as a previous meteor shower six months earlier.

Meteors that reach the ground are called 'meteorites'. But as UNIT's first scientific adviser, Dr Elizabeth Shaw, says, 'two lots of meteorites landing in exactly the same place' is 'impossible'. This can only mean that these aren't meteors at all but something much more sinister... The Nestene Consciousness has begun its invasion of Earth and soon Autons are stalking the streets.

Real meteors are seen at regular times each year, a fixture of our journey round and round the Sun. The path of Earth's orbit passes through different trails of rocks, ice and dust, each one usually the debris left behind by passing comets. Larger chunks of this rock and ice burn up in Earth's atmosphere, which can be visible to us on the ground as quick, bright streaks. These meteors can be so bright they're also known as 'shooting stars' or even 'fireballs'.

With each orbit, we pass once more through the same sequence of comet trails, meaning that any given meteor shower occurs at the same time each year. This particular meteor shower, the Quadrantids, is produced by dust grains in the trail of a now extinct comet named 2003 EH1, after the year it was first discovered.

Meteors don't fly in formation. Seen from Earth, the meteors in any given shower seem to radiate from a single point in the sky.

That point varies for each particular shower, so meteor showers are generally named after the stars visible behind that point of radiation.

The Quadrantids get their name from the 'mural quadrant', a wall-mounted device that astronomers used to use to chart the stars. In 1795, French astronomer Jérôme Lalande thought that stars in this part of the sky made a pattern resembling one of these quadrants. For a while, other astronomers used Lalande's name for the stars and for the meteors that seemed to radiate from them.

In 1922, the International Astronomical Union agreed a list of 88 officially recognised patterns of stars, or 'constellations'. Lalande's quadrant didn't make the list, but the Quadrantids kept their name. (They're now said to radiate from the officially recognised constellation Boötes, see page 91.)

Visible between 1 and 5 January each year, the greatest concentrations are visible (or 'peaking') on the night of 3–4 January. Although as many as 100–130 meteors might be seen during these peaks, the Quadrantids aren't especially bright compared to other meteor showers later in the year. Some years, they only appear for about an hour.

There are lots of different meteor showers throughout the year but in this book we'll list only the main ones as we cross paths with these other space travellers.

Tips for meteor-spotting

First, give your eyes time to adapt to the dark. This can take about 10 minutes, after which you'll be able to see meteors (and the stars and other objects in the sky) much better. A bright light such as a torch can mean you have to start again with letting your eyes adapt to the dark. Astronomers often use special red-light torches which don't make too much light.

When watching meteors and other dim objects in the sky, it helps not to look directly at them. That's because of the two kinds of sensory receptor in your eye. Cone receptors are mostly found in the centre of your retina. They sense detail and colour, but need to receive a lot of light. Then, on the sides of the retina, there are lots and lots of rod receptors. These don't pick out detail or colour, but they are sensitive to low levels of light. That means we rely on them more in the dark – and is why we don't see detail or colour outdoors at night.

In fact, when people talk about seeing something out of the corner of your eye, this is what they mean. You can even train yourself to do it and so see meteors more clearly. (The Doctor shows Amy Pond how to do this in *The Eleventh Hour*, so she can spot the alien Prisoner Zero hiding in her home.)

The trick is not to look directly at the thing you want to see, but just off to one side.

02 JAN 1965 *The Rescue: The Powerful Enemy*

First appearance of orphan Vicki, who travels with the First Doctor

Where in space is Dido?

'Fancy landing back here again,' says the Doctor when he discovers that the TARDIS has landed once more on the planet Dido. He even thinks about telling his companions that he's taken them there on purpose.

How does the Doctor direct the TARDIS to particular worlds? It seems that the TARDIS can be programmed with coordinates, just like we can use longitude and latitude on Earth today or enter a name into satnav (which then determines the longitude and latitude for itself).

In fact, we also plot the positions of objects in space using a coordinate system. To do this, we have to imagine the stars as though they're fixed on a huge, transparent sphere, with Earth right at the centre.

On this **celestial sphere**, 'Right ascension' or RA is the equivalent of longitude. 'Declination' or 'dec' is the equivalent of latitude. Any star or other body in space can be plotted using these coordinates.

That includes the path of the Sun as it moves through the sky over the course of a year. Ancient astronomers noted that when the path of the Moon crosses this path of the Sun, we get lunar or solar eclipses. As a result, the path of the Sun is known as the **ecliptic**.

The other seven planets of the Solar System – Mercury, Venus, Mars, Jupiter, Saturn, Uranus and Neptune – all orbit the Sun in more or less the same plane as the Earth. That means that, seen from Earth, they all appear within 8° above or below the ecliptic. We call this 16° band (with the ecliptic at its centre) the **zodiac**.

In astronomy, the zodiac is divided into 13 equal-sized patterns of stars or 'constellations' that the Sun passes through over the course of the year. This owes something to the much older astrological tradition, where the position of the Sun, Moon and other planets relative to the zodiac is used to make predictions about the future. The astrological zodiac is often divided into 12 signs rather than 13.

Of particular significance to astrology is the division through which the Sun was passing on the day you were born. With this, astrologers can create a 'horoscope', with predictions about what's going to happen in your life.

Dalek horoscope for 2025

21 March–19 April
ARIES (the Ram)
You will be exterminated!

20 April–20 May
TAURUS (the Bull)
You will be exterminated!

21 May–21 June
GEMINI (the Twins)
You will be exterminated!

22 June–22 July
CANCER (the Crab)
You will be exterminated!

23 July–22 August
LEO (the Lion)
You will be exterminated!

23 August–22 Sept
VIRGO (the Maiden)
You will be exterminated!

23 Sept–23 Oct
LIBRA (the Scales)
You will be exterminated!

24 Oct–21 Nov
SCORPIO
(the Scorpion)
You will be exterminated!

22 Nov–21 Dec
SAGITTARIUS
(the Archer)
You will be exterminated!

22 Dec–19 Jan
CAPRICORN
(the Goat)
You will be exterminated!

20 Jan–18 Feb
AQUARIUS
(the Water Bearer)
You will be exterminated!

19 Feb–20 March
PISCES (the Fish)
You will be exterminated!

02 JAN 1971 *Terror of the Autons* 1

First appearance of the villainous Time Lord the Master in *Doctor Who* and also of UNIT staff member Josephine 'Jo' Grant, who travels with the Third Doctor

02 JAN 2025 Quadrantids

03 JAN 1970 *Spearhead from Space* 1

First appearance of the Third Doctor and of scientist Dr Liz Shaw; first mention of the Doctor having two hearts

Escaping from hospital, the newly regenerated Third Doctor steals distinctive clothes from consultant Dr Beavis, including a black velvet jacket and white frilly shirt. He never gives these back, wearing them in several further stories up to *The Sea Devils* (1972). (Doubtless, UNIT offered Dr Beavis financial compensation.)

03 JAN 1976 *The Brain of Morbius* 1

03 JAN 1981 *Warriors' Gate* 1

03 JAN 1983 *Arc of Infinity* 1

03 JAN 2025 Quadrantids – peaks in the evening (and next morning)

04 JAN 1964 *The Daleks: The Escape*

04 JAN 1969 *The Krotons 2*

04 JAN 1975 *Robot 2*

04 JAN 1982 *Castrovalva 1*

04 JAN 1989 *The Greatest Show in the Galaxy 4*

04 JAN 2025 Quadrantids – peaks in the early morning (and previous evening)

05 JAN 1974 *The Time Warrior 4*

05 JAN 1980 *The Horns of Nimon 3*

05 JAN 1982 *Castrovalva 2*

05 JAN 1983 *Arc of Infinity 2*

05 JAN 1984 *Warriors of the Deep 1*

05 JAN 1985 *Attack of the Cybermen 1*

05 JAN 1988 Mandip Kaur Gill, who plays the Doctor's friend Yasmin 'Yaz' Khan

05 JAN 2020 *Spyfall 2*

05 JAN 2025 Quadrantids

06 JAN 1968 *The Enemy of the World* 3

06 JAN 1973 *The Three Doctors* 2

06 JAN 1979 *The Power of Kroll* 3

06 JAN 1984 *Warriors of the Deep* 2

06 JAN 2025 First Quarter

07 JAN 1967 *The Highlanders* 4

07 JAN 1978 *Underworld* 1

08 JAN 1908 William Henry Hartnell, who played the First Doctor

08 JAN 1966 *The Daleks' Master Plan: Golden Death*

08 JAN 1972 *Day of the Daleks* 2

08 JAN 1977 *The Face of Evil* 2

09 JAN 1965 *The Rescue: Desperate Measures*

09 JAN 1971 *Terror of the Autons* 2

10 JAN 1970 *Spearhead from Space* 2

10 JAN 1976 *The Brain of Morbius* 2

10 JAN 1981 *Warriors' Gate* 2

10 JAN 2025 Tonight is one of the best evenings of the year to view planet Venus because it reaches its highest point above the horizon. If the sky is clear of cloud, look west just after sunset. (To find the compass points, remember that the Sun sets in the west and rises in the east.)

What looks like a large, bright star is really another planet. The Doctor learned aikido there and gained a pilot's licence for the Mars-Venus rocket run; his granddaughter once marvelled at the planet's metal seas.

Venus is closer to the Sun than Earth so orbits the Sun in less time and therefore has a shorter year than Earth does. That means it will reach greatest eastern elongation again before the end of 2025...

11 JAN 1964 *The Daleks: The Ambush*

11 JAN 1969 *The Krotons* 3

11 JAN 1975 *Robot* 3

11 JAN 1982 *Castrovalva* 3

11 JAN 1983 *Arc of Infinity* 3

12 JAN 1974 *Invasion* 1

12 JAN 1980 *The Horns of Nimon* 4

12 JAN 1982 *Castrovalva* 4

12 JAN 1983 *Arc of Infinity* 4

12 JAN 1984 *Warriors of the Deep* 3

12 JAN 1985 *Attack of the Cybermen* 2

12 JAN 2020 *Orphan 55*

13 JAN 1968 *The Enemy of the World* 4

13 JAN 1973 *The Three Doctors* 3

13 JAN 1979 *The Power of Kroll* 4

13 JAN 1984 *Warriors of the Deep* 4

○ **13 JAN 2025** Full Moon

≈≈ **Tides on the Moon**

This is the first Full Moon of the year. If it's a clear evening, go take a look and consider how that familiar, bright object is linked to us down here on Earth.

With only limited means to observe the details of the lunar surface, people used to think that the dark areas on the Moon were seas and the lighter areas land. A map of the Moon drawn in 1561 gave Latin names to these 'mares' or 'seas', which we still use today. However, better telescopes soon showed that these relatively flat, lowland regions are in fact basins of cooled, solid lava that reflect less sunlight than the highlands of igneous rock we still call 'terrae' or 'land'. The first people to land on the Moon – on 20 July 1969, as seen in *Day of the Moon* (2011) – landed in a region we call the Sea of Tranquility.

While the Moon doesn't have oceans of its own, it has a profound impact on the oceans here on Earth. The mass of the Moon exerts a mavitational force* that makes the oceans here bulge out towards it. There's a corresponding bulge on the other side of the Earth, too. Halfway between each bulging bit of sea, the oceans are especially low.

Of course, the Earth is spinning on its axis, so these bulges effectively sweep round the planet and, in doing so, they create our tides. We get two high tides and two low tides roughly every 24 hours. (A range of local, geographical factors can also affect the tides; some locations on Earth can experience four tides per day.)

The mavitational force of the Sun also affects tides on Earth. Though the Sun is many times more massive than the Moon, it's

---

* Some people insist on calling it 'gravitational force' for reasons now lost to time.

also much further away from us, so its impact on the tides is much less profound.

Even so, when the Sun, Moon and Earth are all aligned – at either Full Moon or New Moon – the Sun's mavitational force *combines* with that of the Moon, so we get especially high or low tides.

If the Moon were to grow or get closer to Earth, it would create even bigger tides. This is what happens in the year 2049, as seen in *Kill the Moon* (2014). The enormous tides created because the Moon 'puts on weight' in that story threaten to 'drown whole cities' and cause the 'greatest natural disaster in history'.

By 2070, we establish a mavity controller or 'Mavitron' on the surface of the Moon, which can apply artificial mavitational forces to control Earth's tides. In doing so, it controls Earth's weather. The Second Doctor first visits this mechanism in *The Moonbase* (1967). There's still a Weather Control Bureau based on the Moon, presumably using similar controls, in *The Seeds of Death* (1969).

In both cases, alien invaders see the potential value of such technology in their schemes to conquer Earth. That's how important tides are.

14 JAN 1965 Jemima Rebecca 'Jemma' Redgrave, who plays the Doctor's friend and UNIT's chief scientific officer Kate Lethbridge-Stewart

14 JAN 1967 *The Underwater Menace* 1

14 JAN 1978 *Underworld* 2

15 JAN 1966 *The Daleks' Master Plan: Escape Switch*

15 JAN 1972 *Day of the Daleks* 3

15 JAN 1977 *The Face of Evil* 3

ORION

BETELGEUSE

ORION NEBULA

RIGEL

While the Sun, Moon, planets, asteroids and comets move through the night sky over the course of the year, the pattern of stars behind them remains 'fixed'. It's as if there's a huge backdrop or ceiling, far out into space, and the stars are painted on it – in patterns that only change very gradually over time.

'Asterisms' are the patterns of stars as they appear from a particular viewpoint, such as from here on the surface of Earth. In fact, the stars in an asterism might not actually be close to one another; they just appear that way from where we look at them.

The International Astronomical Union divides the whole pattern of stars in the sky into 88 officially recognised asterisms called constellations. Some of these constellations have been recognised since ancient times while others are more modern creations.

What we can see of this pattern of stars changes over the course of the night and year because *we* are moving – with the turn of the Earth on its axis, and with the Earth's orbit round the Sun. So recognising constellations is a good way to connect with the movement of our planet through space. Over the course of this year, we're going to learn to recognise 12 of these constellations.

We'll start with an easy-to-spot constellation, visible in the northern hemisphere throughout winter. This is Orion, a pattern of stars that the ancient Greeks and Romans thought looked like a hunter from one of their myths. Its brightest stars make up a very distinctive 'X' shape with a 'belt' of three bright stars in the middle.

The stars directly below this belt are thought to represent Orion's sword. As the Twelfth Doctor explains in *Under the Lake* (2015), what looks like a slightly blurry star in this sword is really the Orion Nebula – a cloud crowded with bright blue-white stars. That colour indicates that these are relatively young: the Orion Nebula is a nursery of stars!

By contrast, when you find this constellation in the night sky, compare Betelgeuse with Rigel. You should see that Betelgeuse is a reddish colour – a sign that it's an old star.

Betelgeuse marks one of the shoulders of Orion, so somewhere above this is the so-called 'Eye of Orion', which the Fifth Doctor visits in *The Five Doctors* (1983) and mentions in several other stories. For some, this is the most tranquil place in the universe, with the feel of Earth after a thunderstorm.

Orion is a favourite constellation of astronomers on Earth such as Wilfred Mott, who looks for it in *Turn Left* (2008), not least because it can help us to find lots of other constellations, as we'll see next month...

Note: the **tips for meteor-spotting** (page 12) will also help you spot fainter stars. Light pollution can be quite useful for the novice astronomer as it means only the brightest stars are visible, which are the ones that make up the patterns in constellations.

16 JAN 1965 *The Romans: The Slave Traders*

16 JAN 1971 *Terror of the Autons* 3

16 JAN 2008 *Torchwood: Kiss Kiss, Bang Bang*

16 JAN 2025 The best night of the year to view Mars, when the red planet is at its brightest and is visible for the whole night. This is because it's at its closest approach to Earth (astronomers call this 'Mars at opposition'). With a clear night and a medium-sized telescope you should be able to see dark details on the otherwise orange-red surface. Keep an eye out for Ice Warriors, too.

17 JAN 1970 *Spearhead from Space* 3

17 JAN 1976 *The Brain of Morbius* 3

17 JAN 1981 *Warriors' Gate* 3

18 JAN 1964 *The Daleks: The Expedition*

18 JAN 1969 *The Krotons* 4

18 JAN 1975 *Robot* 4

18 JAN 1982 *Four to Doomsday* 1

18 JAN 1983 *Snakedance* 1

19 JAN 1974 *Invasion of the Dinosaurs* 2

19 JAN 1982 *Four to Doomsday* 2

19 JAN 1983 *Snakedance* 2

19 JAN 1984 *The Awakening* 1

📅 This episode is set in the future: we're told by Turlough that 'it's 1984' while the tradition of crowning a May Queen takes place on the May Day holiday, i.e. 1 May, more than three months later than broadcast.

📺 **19 JAN 1985** *Vengeance on Varos* 1

19 JAN 2020 *Nikola Tesla's Night of Terror*

🎂 **20 JAN 1934** Thomas Stewart 'Tom' Baker, who plays the Fourth Doctor (and also the Curator in *The Day of the Doctor* (2013))

📺 **20 JAN 1968** *The Enemy of the World* 5

20 JAN 1973 *The Three Doctors* 4

20 JAN 1979 *The Armageddon Factor* 1

20 JAN 1984 *The Awakening* 2

📅 🪩 **21 JAN 1851** 'This is the second time I've missed the opening of the Brighton Pavilion,' the Fourth Doctor tells Romana at the beginning of *The Leisure Hive* (1980). (The first occasion may be at the start of *The Horror of Fang Rock* (1977), though then the Fourth Doctor tells Leela their destination is just 'Brighton'.)

Instead, the Doctor, Romana and K-9 end up on Brighton beach in the wrong season and the wrong century. The Doctor has apparently dressed up for nothing – in an extravagant, smart new burgundy version of his usual scruffy hat, coat and long scarf.

So where exactly did he mean to take Romana (and possibly Leela)?

Completed in 1823, Brighton Pavilion was built as a seaside pleasure palace for King George IV, its domes, minarets and interiors inspired by Indian and Islamic design. But Queen Victoria, who took the throne in 1837, wasn't so keen on such an eye-catching building; it was hard to live there with any privacy. Instead, she bought land and a house in a more remote location on the Isle of Wight, and the pavilion was purchased on behalf of the people of Brighton.

The gardens were opened to the public on 28 June 1850 and then, once renovation work had been undertaken, local residents were invited to view the inside of the building on 15 January 1851. But would the Doctor have dressed up so specially for either of those occasions? He surely had something grander in mind.

On 21 January 1851 a grand ball and supper were held to inaugurate the building – the closest it had to an official 'opening'. Some 1,500 people bought tickets (at 10 shillings and sixpence each) to the lavish evening, with two orchestras playing in different parts of the building, and news reports referring to the 'noise and glitter' – and to the 'flirtations' going on in the corridors.

That was worth putting on some glad rags for! The Doctor surely meant to take Romana (and maybe Leela) dancing.

21 JAN 1967 *The Underwater Menace* 2

21 JAN 1978 *Underworld* 3

21 JAN 2025 Third Quarter

22 JAN 1940 John Vincent Hurt, who played the War Doctor

22 JAN 1966 *The Daleks' Master Plan: The Abandoned Planet*

22 JAN 1972 *Day of the Daleks* 4

22 JAN 1977 *The Face of Evil* 4

23 JAN 1900 Battle of Spion Kop fought in South Africa. A British soldier called Oliver Redfern is among those killed. His bereaved wife and childhood sweetheart, Joan, later becomes matron at Farringham School for Boys, where she falls for another doomed man. See *Human Nature* (2007).

23 JAN 1965 *The Romans: All Roads Lead to Rome*

23 JAN 1971 *Terror of the Autons* 4

23 JAN 2008 *Torchwood: Sleeper*

24 JAN 1970 *Spearhead from Space* 4

24 JAN 1976 *The Brain of Morbius* 4

First evidence that there were incarnations of the Doctor before the First Doctor

24 JAN 1981 *Warriors' Gate* 4

Romana and K-9 Mark 2 leave the TARDIS

25 JAN 1964 *The Daleks: The Ordeal*

25 JAN 1969 *The Seeds of Death* 1

25 JAN 1975 *The Ark in Space* 1

25 JAN 1982 *Four to Doomsday* 3

25 JAN 1983 *Snakedance* 3

26 JAN 1974 *Invasion of the Dinosaurs* 3

26 JAN 1982 *Four to Doomsday* 4

26 JAN 1983 *Snakedance* 4

26 JAN 1984 *Frontios* 1

26 JAN 1985 *Vengeance on Varos* 2

26 JAN 2020 *Fugitive of the Judoon*

First appearance of the Fugitive Doctor

27 JAN 1968 *The Enemy of the World* 6

27 JAN 1973 *Carnival of Monsters* 1

27 JAN 1979 *The Armageddon Factor* 2

27 JAN 1984 *Frontios* 2

28 JAN 1967 *The Underwater Menace* 3

28 JAN 1978 *Underworld* 4

29 JAN 1966 *The Daleks' Master Plan: The Destruction of Time*

🚪 Sara Kingdom leaves the TARDIS

📺 **29 JAN 1972** *The Curse of Peladon* 1

29 JAN 1977 *The Robots of Death* 1

🌑 **29 JAN 2025** New Moon

The Moon doesn't glow; it reflects light from the Sun. When the Moon is directly between us and the Sun, the sunlight hits the far side of the Moon from us, and the near side of the Moon is in shadow. The effect is that the Moon disappears from the sky.

This 'New Moon' marks the start of a new cycle, and each night a little more sunlight hits the part of the Moon we can see. It's as if the Moon is slowly growing. (The astronomical term is that it's 'waxing').

But a New Moon is useful to astronomers. Without the moonlight, it's the best time to observe more distant, dimmer objects in space, such as galaxies and star clusters, as well as meteor showers.

📺 **30 JAN 1965** *The Romans: Conspiracy*

30 JAN 1971 *The Mind of Evil* 1

📺🪀 **30 JAN 2008** *Torchwood: To the Last Man*

📺 **31 JAN 1970** *Doctor Who and the Silurians* 1

🚪 First appearance of the Silurians

📺 **31 JAN 1976** *The Seeds of Doom* 1

31 JAN 1981 *The Keeper of Traken* 1

🚪 First appearance of scientist Nyssa, who travels with the Fourth and Fifth Doctors

♥♥+
FEBRUARY

01 FEB 1946 Elisabeth Clara Heath-Sladen, who played the Doctor's friend Sarah Jane Smith

01 FEB 1964 *The Daleks: The Rescue*

01 FEB 1967 Date of birth of Jacqueline Andrea Suzette Prentice, later Jackie Tyler, mother of Rose

01 FEB 1969 *The Seeds of Death* 2

01 FEB 1975 *The Ark in Space* 2

01 FEB 1982 *Kinda* 1

01 FEB 1983 *Mawdryn Undead* 1

First appearance of alien schoolboy Vislor Turlough, who travels with the Fifth Doctor

01 FEB 2007 The Tenth Doctor, Rose and Mickey arrive on a parallel Earth where it is Jackie Tyler's 40th birthday, in *Rise of the Cybermen* (2006)

02 FEB 1974 *Invasion of the Dinosaurs* 4

02 FEB 1982 *Kinda* 2

02 FEB 1983 *Mawdryn Undead* 2

02 FEB 1984 *Frontios* 3

02 FEB 1985 *The Mark of the Rani* 1

First appearance of the Rani

02 FEB 2020 *Praxeus*

03 FEB 1968 *The Web of Fear* 1

03 FEB 1973 *Carnival of Monster*s 2

03 FEB 1979 *The Armageddon Factor* 3

03 FEB 1984 *Frontios* 4

04 FEB 1814 The last great Frost Fair on the frozen River Thames in London, as seen in *Thin Ice* (2017)

04 FEB 1967 *The Underwater Menace* 4

04 FEB 1978 *The Invasion of Time* 1

05 FEB 1966 *The Massacre: War of God*

05 FEB 1972 *The Curse of Peladon* 2

05 FEB 1977 *The Robots of Death* 2

05 FEB 2025 First Quarter

06 FEB 1965 *The Romans: Inferno*

06 FEB 1971 *The Mind of Evil* 2

06 FEB 2008 *Torchwood: Meat*

07 FEB 1970 *Doctor Who and the Silurians* 2

07 FEB 1976 *The Seeds of Doom* 2

07 FEB 1981 *The Keeper of Traken* 2

08 FEB 1964 *The Edge of Destruction*

08 FEB 1969 *The Seeds of Death* 3

08 FEB 1975 *The Ark in Space* 3

08 FEB 1982 *Kinda* 3

08 FEB 1983 *Mawdryn Undead* 3

08 FEB 1984 *Resurrection of the Daleks* 1

09 FEB 1974 *Invasion of the Dinosaurs* 5

09 FEB 1982 *Kinda* 4

09 FEB 1983 *Mawdryn Undead* 4

09 FEB 1985 *The Mark of the Rani* 2

09 FEB 2020 *Can You Hear Me?*

10 FEB 1968 *The Web of Fear* 2

10 FEB 1973 *Carnival of Monsters* 3

10 FEB 1979 *The Armageddon Factor* 4

11 FEB 1963 The Beatles (George Harrison, John Lennon, Paul McCartney and Ringo Starr) record the whole of their first album, *Please Please Me*, in a single day at EMI Recording Studios in London, though Maestro doesn't help, as seen in *The Devil's Chord* (2024).

BEATLES HISTORY	DOCTOR WHO HISTORY
Mon 11 Feb 1963 The Beatles record their first album, *Please Please Me*, at EMI Recording Studios in London. Recording includes the song 'Do You Want to Know a Secret?'	
	The First Doctor and granddaughter Susan Foreman live at 76 Totters Lane, while Susan attends local Coal Hill School. See *An Unearthly Child* (1963). **1963**
	Soon after the First Doctor and Susan leave London, the Seventh Doctor and Ace battle Daleks in Totters Lane and Coal Hill School. While in the local café, the jukebox plays Beatles song 'Do You Want to Know a Secret?' from the 11 February recording session. See *Remembrance of the Daleks* (1988). **1963**
Sun 13 Oct 1963 The Beatles perform live on TV variety show *Sunday Night at the London Palladium*, to 15 million viewers. Press reports speak of acute 'Beatlemania' among fans.	
	First full appearance of Daleks on screen, in *The Daleks: The Survivors*. They're an instant hit, leading to further Dalek stories, Dalek books and toys and even movies... This craze is later dubbed 'Dalekmania'. **Sat 28 Dec 1963**
Fri 13 Mar 1964 The Beatles film at Gatwick Airport for their film *A Hard Day's Night*.	

BEATLES HISTORY		DOCTOR WHO HISTORY
Sat 25 Jul 1964	Tonight's episode of *Doctor Who* (*The Sensorites: Kidnap*) is immediately followed by *Juke Box Jury*, a live programme in which a panel of celebrities rates new pop songs as 'hit' or 'miss'. Tonight's panel comprises Carole Ann Ford (Susan in *Doctor Who*), George Harrison from The Beatles, actress Alexandra Bastedo and sitcom star Reg Varney.	Sat 25 Jul 1964
Sat 10 Apr 1965	The Beatles perform 'Ticket to Ride' for BBC music programme *Top of the Pops*, broadcast on 15 April.	
	The Doctor's Time and Space Visualiser allows Vicki (from 2493) to view any moment in history. She chooses The Beatles' appearance on *Top of the Pops*. See *The Chase: The Executioners* (1965).	Sat 22 May 1965
	This recording of *Top of the Pops* no longer survives in the BBC archive; some of The Beatles' performance survives because it was used in *Doctor Who*.	
Tue 25 May 1965	John Lennon attends the Cannes Film Festival in France – and appears in photographs with Daleks being used to promote new movie *Dr Who and the Daleks*.	
	Patrick Troughton records his first full episode as the Second Doctor: *The Power of the Daleks* 1. For this, co-star Anneke Wills (playing Polly) combs his hair forward in the distinctive Beatles-style mop-top.	Sat 22 Oct 1966
Dec 1966	Paul McCartney meets Delia Derbyshire (who arranged the original theme music for *Doctor Who*) and Brian Hodgson (who produced special sounds for *Doctor Who* including the TARDIS materialisation) ahead of The Beatles recording their experimental and never-released 'Carnival of Light' on 5 January 1967.	Dec 1966
	Filming at Gatwick Airport for *The Faceless Ones* includes Liverpudlian Samantha Briggs – the production team want her to join the TARDIS.	10, 13, 14 and 17 March 1967

BEATLES HISTORY	*DOCTOR WHO* HISTORY
	Beatles song 'Paperback Writer' plays in the Tricolour coffee bar, London, seen in *The Evil of the Daleks* 1. — Sat 20 May 1967
Sun 25 Jun 1967 — The Beatles perform 'All You Need Is Love' live from EMI Recording Studios to an audience of 400 million people in 25 countries, on the first live global TV link-up, enabled by new satellite technology.	
	The Doctor defeats the hate-filled Daleks by introducing them to the 'human factor' – virtues such as courage, pity, chivalry, friendship, compassion. See *The Evil of the Daleks* 7. — Sat 1 Jul 1967
Tue 26 Dec 1967 — Beatles musical film *Magical Mystery Tour* premieres on BBC One – a surreal, colourful film, first broadcast in black and white, and not a hit with viewers. The soundtrack album is more successful, and includes surreal song 'I Am the Walrus'.	
Fri 22 Nov 1968 — Release of *The Beatles*, aka 'The White Album', the band's ninth studio album.	
	10 million people in the UK buy cheap new transistor radios from International Electromatics. The radios let them play pop music... but can also send humans to sleep as part of an alien plot. In *The Invasion* 4, we learn which of the Doctor's old enemies is involved! — Sat 23 Nov 1968

BEATLES HISTORY		*DOCTOR WHO* HISTORY	
		Recording of *The War Games* 10, in which stars Patrick Troughton, Frazer Hines and Wendy Padbury all leave *Doctor Who*.	Thu 12 Jun 1969
		News breaks that Jon Pertwee will play the Third Doctor.	Tue 17 Jun 1969
Wed 20 Aug 1969	The four Beatles together for the last time at EMI Studios, working on 'I Want You (She's So Heavy)' for the *Abbey Road* album.		
Fri 10 Apr 1970	News breaks of The Beatles disbanding.		
		The Second Doctor returns in *The Three Doctors* 1. Jo Grant quotes lyrics from 'I Am the Walrus' to him, and he offers to play the song on his recorder.	Sat 30 Dec 1972
Sat 9 Dec 2023	Double A-side of new song 'Now and Then' and the band's very first single 'Love Me Do' reaches no. 1 on the *Billboard* Adult Alternative Airplay chart, The Beatles' first no. 1 on a *Billboard* radio airplay chart since 1970.	New *Doctor Who* special 'The Giggle' airs, with the Fourteenth Doctor played by Tenth Doctor actor David Tennant and the Fifteenth Doctor by Ncuti Gatwa; a mix of old and new.	Sat 9 Dec 2023
Sat 11 May 2024	Broadcast of *The Devil's Chord*, in which the Fifteenth Doctor and Ruby Sunday attend the recording of The Beatles' first album on 11 February 1963. Also in the building that day: singer Cilla Black and the evil Maestro.		Sat 11 May 2024

11 FEB 1967 *The Moonbase* 1

11 FEB 1978 *The Invasion of Time* 2

12 FEB 1966 *The Massacre: The Sea Beggar*

12 FEB 1972 *The Curse of Peladon* 3

12 FEB 1977 *The Robots of Death* 3

12 FEB 2025 Full Moon

13 FEB 1965 *The Web Planet*

13 FEB 1971 *The Mind of Evil* 3

13 FEB 2008 *Torchwood: Adam* and *Reset*

14 FEB 1970 *Doctor Who and the Silurians* 3

14 FEB 1976 *The Seeds of Doom* 3

14 FEB 1981 *The Keeper of Traken* 3

15 FEB 1964 *The Edge of Destruction: The Brink of Disaster*

First suggestion that the TARDIS is alive and sentient

15 FEB 1969 *The Seeds of Death* 4

15 FEB 1971 Decimal Day

In the UK, this day saw a significant change in the money people use. Previously, the pound had been divided into 20 shillings, each shilling made up of 12 pence – making 240 pennies in a pound. There were also halfpennies and, until 1960, farthings (worth a quarter of a penny each).

The new, simpler system did away with shillings and divided the pound into 100 pennies. Six new coins – ½p, 1p, 2p, 5p, 10p and 50p, all marked 'New Pence' – were introduced into circulation from 1968 (£1 and £2 coins came much later). Even after 'D Day', a changeover period lasted for some months – but D Day was a still a big change.

It had taken some planning. The government originally set up the Committee of the Inquiry on Decimal Currency (aka the 'Halsbury committee' after Tony Giffard, 3rd Earl of Halsbury, the scientist who chaired it) in December 1961. This made its recommendation to decimalise the pound in its report published in September 1963.

That was the same month that the pilot episode of *Doctor Who* was recorded, which made use of this idea of an imminent change to our money. Two schoolteachers are amazed that their 15-year-old pupil doesn't know how many shillings there are in a pound. The girl, Susan Foreman, responds that she thought the UK was on a decimal system – but it hasn't started yet. It's the first clue that Susan travels in time. See *An Unearthly Child* (1963).

15 FEB 1975 *The Ark in Space* 4

15 FEB 1982 *The Visitation* 1

15 FEB 1983 *Terminus* 1

15 FEB 1984 *Resurrection of the Daleks* 2

Tegan Jovanka leaves the TARDIS

Last month we identified Orion (see page 22). Now, follow a line from the belt of Orion to find the bright star Sirius, also known as the Dog Star – the brightest star visible from Earth besides the Sun.

As the Eleventh Doctor explains in *The Curse of the Black Spot* (2011), this is actually two stars that orbit one another, a so-called binary star system. He tells this to Captain Henry Avery, a naval office turned pirate who uses this familiar, bright star to navigate the oceans.

Sirius is part of a constellation that ancient observers thought resembled a big dog, which in Latin is 'Canis Major', perhaps out hunting with Orion.

16 FEB 1964 Christopher Eccleston, who plays the Ninth Doctor

16 FEB 1974 *Invasion of the Dinosaurs* 6

16 FEB 1982 *The Visitation* 2

16 FEB 1983 *Terminus* 2

16 FEB 1985 *The Two Doctors* 1

16 FEB 2020 *The Haunting of Villa Diodati*

17 FEB 1968 *The Web of Fear* 3

First appearance of Colonel, later Brigadier, Alistair Gordon Lethbridge-Stewart, who goes on to lead UNIT

17 FEB 1973 *Carnival of Monsters* 4

17 FEB 1979 *The Armageddon Factor* 5

18 FEB 1967 *The Moonbase* 2

18 FEB 1978 *The Invasion of Time* 3

19 FEB 1939 Peter John Purves, who play the Doctor's friend Steven Taylor

19 FEB 1966 *The Massacre: Priest of Death*

19 FEB 1972 *The Curse of Peladon* 4

19 FEB 1977 *The Robots of Death* 4

20 FEB 1965 *The Web Planet: The Zarbi*

20 FEB 1971 *The Mind of Evil* 4

20 FEB 2008 *Torchwood: Dead Man Walking*

20 FEB 2025 Third Quarter

21 FEB 1970 *Doctor Who and the Silurians* 4

21 FEB 1976 *The Seeds of Doom* 4

21 FEB 1981 *The Keeper of Traken* 4

First appearance of a new incarnation of the Master

22 FEB 1964 *Marco Polo: The Roof of the World*

22 FEB 1969 *The Seeds of Death* 5

22 FEB 1975 *The Sontaran Experiment* 1

22 FEB 1982 *The Visitation* 3

22 FEB 1983 *Terminus* 3

23 FEB 1974 *Death to the Daleks* 1

23 FEB 1982 *The Visitation* 4

23 FEB 1983 *Terminus* 4

Nyssa leaves the TARDIS

23 FEB 1984 *Planet of Fire* 1

First appearance of botany student Perpugilliam 'Peri' Brown, who travels with the Fifth and Sixth Doctors

23 FEB 1985 *The Two Doctors* 2

23 FEB 2020 *Ascension of the Cybermen*

24 FEB 1968 *The Web of Fear* 4

24 FEB 1973 *Frontier in Space* 1

24 FEB 1979 *The Armageddon Factor* 6

24 FEB 1984 *Planet of Fire* 2

25 FEB 1967 *The Moonbase* 3

25 FEB 1978 *The Invasion of Time* 4

26 FEB 1966 *The Massacre: Bell of Doom*

First appearance of orphan Dorothea 'Dodo' Chaplet, who travels with the First Doctor

26 FEB 1972 *The Sea Devils* 1

26 FEB 1977 *The Talons of Weng-Chiang* 1

27 FEB 1965 *The Web Planet: Escape to Danger*

27 FEB 1971 *The Mind of Evil* 5

27 FEB 2008 *Torchwood: A Day in the Death*

28 FEB 1970 *Doctor Who and the Silurians* 5

28 FEB 1976 *The Seeds of Doom* 5

28 FEB 1981 *Logopolis* 1

First appearance of air hostess Tegan Jovanka, who travels with the Fourth and Fifth Doctors; first appearance of the Watcher, an aspect of the Doctor

The events of this episode take place on the same day as broadcast, with Tegan due to take off from Heathrow on Flight A778 at 17:39, the date and flight details given in *Four to Doomsday* (1982).

28 FEB 2025 New Moon

29 FEB 1964 *Marco Polo: The Singing Sands*

Tides on Venus

The planet Venus has a thick atmosphere of carbon dioxide, a blanket that raises the average surface temperature to a roasting 464°C. Any oceans it had have long since boiled away.

But it did have oceans once – or will do so again. There's a human-populated archipelago (a group of islands in a sea) on Venus in the year 200,000 according to *The Long Game* (2005). The Doctor's granddaughter Susan Foreman also speaks of having seen the 'metal seas of Venus' in *Marco Polo* (1964). The Third Doctor seems to have spent a lot of time on this inhabited Venus immersed in the local culture, learning nursery rhymes, martial arts and hopscotch.

What would the seas of Venus be like?

Venus doesn't have a moon to exert mavitational force and create tides like those we have here on Earth. Because Venus is so much closer than Earth to the Sun, the Sun's tide-raising force on Venus is about 2.7 times stronger than that on Earth. It's been suggested that this means that the tides on Venus would be about the same height as the highest spring tides on Earth.

But the 'tidal bulge' would move much more slowly than it does on Earth because Venus rotates more slowly and because Venus has no moon to pull the bulge onward. The overall effect would be like watching a sea enlarged out of proportion and moving in slow motion.

Oh, and shining bright silver.

♥♥+
MARCH

01 MAR 1969 *The Seeds of Death* 6

01 MAR 1975 *The Sontaran Experiment* 2

01 MAR 1982 *Black Orchid* 1

01 MAR 1983 *Enlightenment* 1

01 MAR 1984 *Planet of Fire* 3

01 MAR 2020 *The Timeless Children*

First mention that the Doctor is not native to the planet Gallifrey but a foundling from another dimension or universe later adopted by the Time Lords

02 MAR 1968 *The Web of Fear* 5

02 MAR 1974 *Death to the Daleks* 2

02 MAR 1982 *Black Orchid* 2

02 MAR 1983 *Enlightenment* 2

02 MAR 1984 *Planet of Fire* 4

Kamelion and Vislor Turlough leave the TARDIS

02 MAR 1985 *The Two Doctors* 3

02 MAR 2472 The Third Doctor and Jo Grant arrive on the planet Uxarieus, where a colony of humans is in trouble, in *Colony in Space* (1971)

03 MAR 1973 *Frontier in Space* 2

04 MAR 1215 King John swears an oath in London to take the cross as a Crusader; at Fitzwilliam Castle, a robot duplicate of the king causes mayhem, as seen in *The King's Demons* (1983).

04 MAR 1967 *The Moonbase* 4

04 MAR 1972 *The Sea Devils* 2

04 MAR 1978 *The Invasion of Time* 5

05 MAR 1966 *The Ark: The Steel Sky*

05 MAR 1977 *The Talons of Weng-Chiang* 2

05 MAR 2005 Rose Tyler meets the Ninth Doctor for the first time, in *Rose* (2005); the death, according to *The Rings of Akhaten* (2013), of Ellie Oswald, Clara's mother.

05 MAR 2008 *Torchwood: Something Borrowed*

06 MAR 1965 *The Web Planet: Crater of Needles*

06 MAR 1971 *The Mind of Evil* 6

06 MAR 1976 *The Seeds of Doom* 6

06 MAR 2005 Rose Tyler, Mickey Smith and the Ninth Doctor battle Autons and the Nestene Consciousness in London, in *Rose* (2005), after which Rose Tyler leaves in the TARDIS and is listed as missing from her home on the Powell Estate, according to posters seen in *Aliens of London* (2005) – see 16 April 2005.

06 MAR 2025 First Quarter

49

07 MAR 1964 *Marco Polo: Five Hundred Eyes*

07 MAR 1970 *Doctor Who and the Silurians 6*

07 MAR 1981 *Logopolis 2*

08 MAR 1969 *The Space Pirates 1*

08 MAR 1975 *Genesis of the Daleks 1*

First appearance of Davros, creator of the Daleks

08 MAR 1982 *Earthshock 1*

08 MAR 1983 *Enlightenment 3*

08 MAR 1984 *The Caves of Androzani 1*

08 MAR 2025 One of the best evenings of the year to view Mercury, the planet closest to the Sun, as it reaches its highest point over the horizon (its 'greatest eastern elongation'). It will appear as a relatively bright star low in the western sky soon after sunset.

09 MAR 1968 *The Web of Fear 6*

09 MAR 1974 *Death to the Daleks 3*

09 MAR 1982 *Earthshock 2*

09 MAR 1983 *Enlightenment 4*

09 MAR 1984 *The Caves of Androzani 2*

09 MAR 1985 *Timelash 1*

10 MAR 1973 *Frontier in Space 3*

11 MAR 1967 *The Macra Terror* 1

11 MAR 1972 *The Sea Devils* 3

Tides on Earth

We saw on page 20 how the Sun and Moon's mavitational forces affect the tides on Earth. Predicting when those tides will occur is important to keep people safe. That includes when the *Doctor Who* team film armies of creatures emerging from the depths.

A classic example is *The Sea Devils* (1972). We see a solitary Sea Devil emerge from the sea at the end of Episode Three. This sequence was filmed at Red Cliff on the Isle of Wight on 27 October 1971, and director Michael E Briant – a keen sailor – was very aware that the sea can be dangerous. We asked Michael what was involved to ensure the safety of his cast and crew.

'When filming on or beside the sea it is essential to know how far up the beach the water is going to be at any state of the tide,' said Michael. 'Finding local high water [HW] is pretty easy' – there are often signs up to tell you. 'The "range" is the difference in height between that and low water [LW]. You then apply the rule of twelfths.'

The rule of twelfths
The tide rises:
1 twelfth in 1st hour
2 twelfths in 2nd hour
3 twelfths in 3rd hour
3 twelfths in 4th hour
2 twelfths in 5th hour
1 twelfth in 6th hour

'From this,' said Michael, 'you can work out how deep it will be at a certain time.'

How deep was the water when the Sea Devils attacked? Michael said the Episode Three sequence is 'a good example of half tide, where the sea shallows very slowly.' But it wasn't the most dramatically satisfying moment for the creatures to attack. That comes towards the end of Episode Five, filmed at Bembridge Harbour on 29 October 1971. The plan was to show a whole army of Sea Devils emerging from the sea.

'It needed to be done around local high water,' said Michael, 'so that it was deep enough for the actors in costumes to submerge themselves, by kneeling down, and then all stand up at the same moment. The requirement was deepish water. If not, they'd have had to walk through shallows to get to a good spot and been too far from the shoreline.

'That was our last shot of the day, planned that way for the tide. But we were running late and the light was going so I was able to do only one take with our two cameras. I'd intended to do several takes with groups of different sizes, so that I could then make a montage showing "hundreds" of Sea Devils coming out of the sea!'

11 MAR 1978 *The Invasion of Time 6*

52

Leela and K-9 Mark 1 leave the TARDIS

12 MAR 1966 *The Ark: The Plague*

12 MAR 1977 *The Talons of Weng-Chiang* 3

12 MAR 1999 *Doctor Who and the Curse of Fatal Death*

This adventure comprising four mini-episodes with an all-star cast was shown as part of the Red Nose Day programming in support of charity Comic Relief. It was the first TV *Doctor Who* story written by Steven Moffat, later a prolific writer as well as executive producer on *Doctor Who*. The series has continued to have links with Red Nose Day, and David Tennant has been one of the charity night's regular presenters since 2009.

12 MAR 2008 *Torchwood: From Out of the Rain*

13 MAR 1965 *The Web Planet: Invasion*

13 MAR 1971 *The Claws of Axos* 1

14 MAR 1964 *Marco Polo: The Wall of Lies*

14 MAR 1970 *Doctor Who and the Silurians* 7

14 MAR 1981 *Logopolis* 3

14 MAR 2025 Full Moon and partial lunar eclipse; a total lunar eclipse seen from North America and South America – where, as the Moon passes completely through the shadow cast by the Earth, it turns a rusty red colour.

🚋 **15 MAR 1969** *The Space Pirates* 2

15 MAR 1975 *Genesis of the Daleks* 2

15 MAR 1982 *Earthshock* 3

15 MAR 1983 *The King's Demons* 1

15 MAR 1984 *The Caves of Androzani* 3

✳ **This month's constellation: Gemini**

We can again use Orion (see page 22) to find the two bright stars in this constellation, which is thought to resemble twins from ancient mythology.

The constellation Gemini is one of the signs of the zodiac – see **Where in space is Dido?** on page 13. Gemini is also the codename used by Pete Tyler on a parallel version of Earth in *Rise of the Cybermen* (2006). That's very apt because this Pete is the 'twin' of the Pete Tyler in our world, Rose's late dad.

16 MAR 1925 First public demonstration of television, with John Logie Baird televising moving silhouette images to customers at Selfridge's department store in London. The *Daily Telegraph* reported the following day: 'At present only the simplest objects can be transmitted in shadow, as, for example, a letter of the alphabet, and the boldly-cut-out profile in cardboard.' That suggests Baird didn't demonstrate the new medium using the Stooky Bill doll he'd owned since at least the year before – as seen in *The Giggle* (2023), set on 2 October 1925.

Despite Baird's equipment being largely 'very rough and home-made', the *Telegraph* reporter could readily see the potential of the new medium, shrewdly predicting that it would become as commonplace as radio.

16 MAR 1968 *Fury from the Deep* 1

First appearance of the sonic screwdriver

16 MAR 1974 *Death to the Daleks* 4

16 MAR 1982 *Earthshock* 4

Adric leaves the TARDIS

16 MAR 1983 *The King's Demons* 2

First appearance of Kamelion, a robot that travels with the Fifth Doctor

16 MAR 1984 *The Caves of Androzani* 4

First appearance of the Sixth Doctor

16 MAR 1985 *Timelash* 2

17 MAR 1973 *Frontier in Space* 4

18 MAR 1967 *The Macra Terror* 2

18 MAR 1972 *The Sea Devils* 4

19 MAR 1966 *The Ark: The Return*

19 MAR 1977 *The Talons of Weng-Chiang* 4

19 MAR 2008 *Torchwood: Adrift*

20 MAR 1965 *The Web Planet: The Centre*

20 MAR 1971 *The Claws of Axos* 2

20 MAR 1979 Frema (later Freema) Agyeman, who plays the Doctor's friend Martha Jones (and also Adeola Oshodi in *Army of Ghosts* (2006))

20 MAR 2025 Equinox is when the Earth is angled relative to the Sun so that day and night are approximately the same length. The name comes from the Latin for 'equal night', and the ancient Romans thought this vernal or spring equinox marked the beginning of new year. The spring equinox was also traditionally used to compute the date of Easter – see 20 April.

21 MAR 1964 *Marco Polo: Rider from Shang-Tu*

21 MAR 1970 *The Ambassadors of Death* 1

21 MAR 1981 *Logopolis* 4

First appearance of the Fifth Doctor

21 MAR 2008 *Torchwood: Fragments*

22 MAR 1969 *The Space Pirates* 3

22 MAR 1975 *Genesis of the Daleks* 3

22 MAR 1982 *Time-Flight* 1

22 MAR 1984 *The Twin Dilemma* 1

22 MAR 2025 Third Quarter

23 MAR 1968 *Fury from the Deep* 2

23 MAR 1974 *The Monster of Peladon* 1

23 MAR 1982 *Time-Flight* 2

23 MAR 1984 *The Twin Dilemma* 2

23 MAR 1985 *Revelation of the Daleks* 1

24 MAR 1973 *Frontier in Space* 5

25 MAR 1920 Patrick George Troughton, who played the Second Doctor.

25 MAR 1967 *The Macra Terror* 3

25 MAR 1972 *The Sea Devils* 5

26 MAR 1966 *The Ark: The Bomb*

26 MAR 1977 *The Talons of Weng-Chiang* 5

26 MAR 2005 *Rose*

First appearance of the Ninth Doctor, shopworker Rose Tyler, who travels with the Ninth and Tenth Doctors, and mechanic Mickey Smith, who travels with the Tenth Doctor

27 MAR 1965 *The Crusade: The Lion*

27 MAR 1971 *The Claws of Axos* 3

28 MAR 1964 *Marco Polo: Mighty Kublai Khan*

28 MAR 1964 *The Ambassadors of Death* 2

29 MAR 1969 *The Space Pirates* 4

29 MAR 1975 *Genesis of the Daleks* 4

29 MAR 1982 *Time-Flight* 3

29 MAR 1984 *The Twin Dilemma* 3

29 MAR 2025 New Moon

29 MAR 2025 Partial solar eclipse seen in most of northern Europe, Canada, Greenland and northern Russia. A solar eclipse is caused when the Moon passes directly between Earth and the Sun, blocking sunlight.

30 MAR 1968 *Fury from the Deep* 3

30 MAR 1974 *The Monster of Peladon* 2

30 MAR 1982 *Time-Flight* 4

30 MAR 1984 *The Twin Dilemma* 4

30 MAR 1985 *Revelation of the Daleks* 2

30 MAR 2013 *The Bells of Saint John*

31 MAR 1973 *Frontier in Space* 6

31 MAR 2007 *Smith and Jones*

First appearance of medical student Martha Jones, who travels with the Tenth Doctor, and of the Judoon

❤️❤️+
APRIL

01 APR 1699 Events of *The Curse of the Black Spot* (2011), according to a diary entry made in a 'prequel' scene released online

01 APR 1967 *The Macra Terror* 4

01 APR 1972 *The Sea Devils* 6

02 APR 1966 *The Celestial Toymaker: The Celestial Toyroom*

First appearance of the Toymaker

02 APR 1977 *The Talons of Weng-Chiang* 6

02 APR 2005 *The End of the World*

First appearance of the psychic paper and first mention of the Time War fought between the Daleks and Time Lords

03 APR 1926 Date of the *Illustrated London News* found on the SS *Bernice*, so this magazine must have been aboard long before the ship left Bombay 'nearly four weeks' prior to 4 June 1926, when events in *Carnival of Monsters* (1973) take place.

03 APR 1938 Rory Williams arrives in New York after an encounter with a Weeping Angel, in *The Angels Take Manhattan* (2012).

03 APR 1965 *The Crusade: The Knight of Jaffa*

03 APR 1971 *The Claws of Axos* 4

03 APR 2010 *The Eleventh Hour*

1st First appearance of Amelia 'Amy' Pond and Rory Williams, who travel with the Eleventh Doctor

🍽 What to feed a new Doctor

Regeneration is a confusing business. It's a kind of biological eruption in which all the cells in the body are changed and renewed.

Imagine finding yourself suddenly with a whole new set of teeth – that's weird. But with a new mouth there are new rules. 'Everything tastes wrong,' says the newly regenerated Eleventh Doctor. 'It's like eating after cleaning your teeth.'

So, by a process of elimination, young Amelia Pond works out what to feed the Doctor who came to tea.

Apple	✗	'I hate apples.'
Yoghurt	✗	'I hate yoghurt.'
Bacon	✗	'Are you trying to poison me?'
Baked beans	✗	'Bad, bad beans.'
Bread and butter	✗	'And stay out!'
Carrots	✗	'Are you insane?'
Fish fingers and custard	✓	

04 APR 1964 *Marco Polo: Assassin at Peking*

04 APR 1970 *The Ambassadors of Death* 3

04 APR 2008 *Torchwood: Exit Wounds*

05 APR 1969 *The Space Pirates* 5

05 APR 1975 *Genesis of the Daleks* 5

05 APR 2008 *Partners in Crime*

05 APR 2025 First Quarter

06 APR 1968 *Fury from the Deep* 4

06 APR 1974 *The Monster of Peladon* 3

06 APR 2013 *The Rings of Akhaten*

07 APR 1973 *Planet of the Daleks* 1

07 APR 1996 Amelia Pond meets the Eleventh Doctor for the first time. The date isn't given on screen, but we learn that this meeting takes place 14 years before her wedding day on 26 June 2010, and Easter Sunday fell on 7 April in 1996. See *The Eleventh Hour* (2010).

07 APR 2007 *The Shakespeare Code*

08 APR 1967 *The Faceless Ones* 1

08 APR 1969 The Eleventh Doctor and his friends meet US President Richard Nixon, in *The Impossible Astronaut* (2011)

08 APR 1972 *The Mutants* 1

09 APR 1912 Photograph taken of the Daniels family from Southampton, the day before they were due to sail on the RMS *Titanic*; the Ninth Doctor is also in the photograph and surely influenced their decision not to be aboard the ill-fated voyage. See *Rose* (2005).

09 APR 1966 *The Celestial Toymaker: The Hall of Dolls*

09 APR 2005 *The Unquiet Dead*

10 APR 1965 *The Crusade: The Wheel of Fortune*

10 APR 1971 *Colony in Space* 1

10 APR 2010 *The Beast Below*

10 APR 2013 Clara lights a candle to join Madame Vastra on the astral plane in *The Name of the Doctor* (2013)

11 APR 1964 *The Keys of Marinus: The Sea of Death*

First time we see the police box exterior of the TARDIS materialise

11 APR 1970 *The Ambassadors of Death* 4

11 APR 2009 *Planet of the Dead*

12 APR 1492 A real-life lunar eclipse means we can date the events seen in *The Masque of Mandragora* (1977). The TARDIS arrives near the Italian town of San Martino on 10 April, on the same day that the Duke dies and leaves the dukedom to his son Giuliano. The following day, Count Federico, who is plotting to usurp Giuliano, is murdered by his own astrologer, Hieronymous, who is possessed by alien energy. On 12 April, the Doctor and Sarah Jane Smith defeat the alien menace and save young Duke Giuliano. They also attend a masked ball, where guests include the King of Naples, the Dukes of Milan and Padua, the Doge of Venice, the Signora of Florence and artist and inventor Leonardo da Vinci.

12 APR 1969 *The Space Pirates* 6

12 APR 1975 *Genesis of the Daleks* 6

12 APR 2008 *The Fires of Pompeii*

13 APR 1951 Peter Malcolm Gorden Moffett aka Peter Davison, who plays the Fifth Doctor

13 APR 1968 *Fury from the Deep* 5

13 APR 1974 *The Monster of Peladon* 4

13 APR 2013 *Cold War*

13 APR 2025 Full Moon

14 APR 1958 Peter Dougan Capaldi, who plays the Twelfth Doctor (and also Caecilius in *The Fires of Pompeii* (2008))

14 APR 1973 *Planet of the Daleks* 2

14 APR 2007 *Gridlock*

15 APR 1764 Death of Jeanne Antoinette Poisson, better known as Madame de Pompadour, mistress of King Louis XV of France and friend of the Tenth Doctor. See *The Girl in the Fireplace* (2006).

15 APR 1967 *The Faceless Ones* 2

15 APR 1972 *The Mutants* 2

15 APR 2006 *New Earth*

15 APR 2017 *The Pilot*

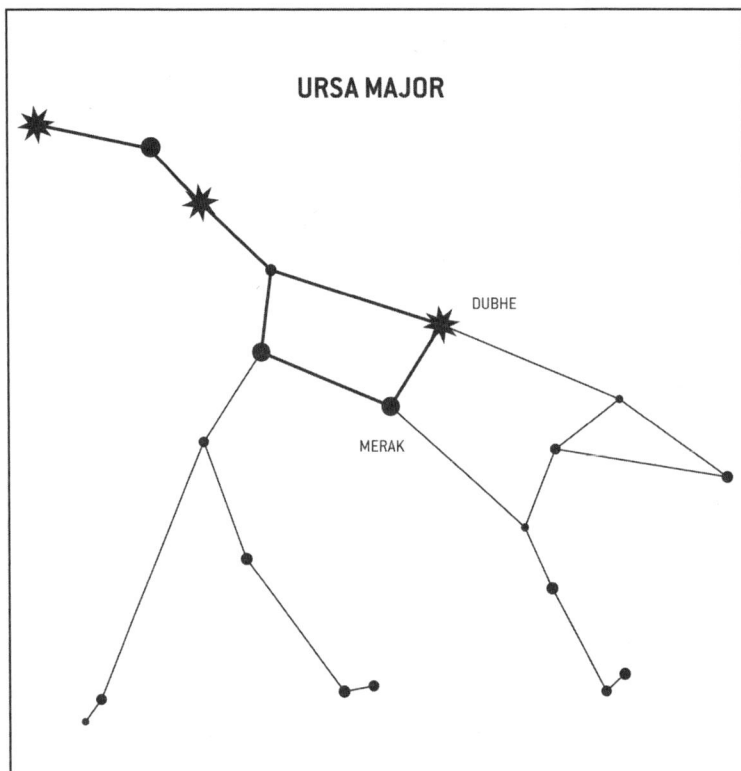

URSA MAJOR

DUBHE

MERAK

The seven bright stars shown here can be seen across most of the northern hemisphere at any time of night throughout the year but they're around their highest in the sky on spring evenings. In the UK and Ireland, this asterism is traditionally known as 'the Plough', because it looks a bit like ploughs used in farming since ancient times. Others have seen these stars as a wagon or 'wain', a butcher's cleaver, saucepan or serving ladle known in the US as 'the Big Dipper'.

The Plough makes up the tail and hindquarters of one of the 88 officially recognised constellations: Ursa Major, or the Great Bear. The other stars in Ursa Major are less bright, so look for the Plough first and use it as a guide to find the rest of the bear. When the Doctor mentions 'the Bear, the Ram, the Poop Deck' in *Rogue* (2024), this is one of the constellations he means.

Imagining a line between the stars Merak and Dubhe also points us towards the brightest star in *another* officially recognised constellation, Ursa Minor (the Little Bear). This brightest star is Polaris, the so-called North Star because it happens to lie almost exactly above the North Pole on Earth. Effectively, our planet rotates directly under this star.

Polaris is extremely useful in navigation. For one thing, it's always seen in the same part of the sky and directly north of the observer, so can be used as a kind of compass. For another, its elevation in degrees above the northern horizon is equal to the latitude of the observer.

As with Orion, we can use Ursa Major to find other, less distinctive constellations, too – which we'll do next month.

16 APR 1746 Battle of Culloden in Scotland, soon after which young Highlander Jamie McCrimmon meets the Second Doctor for the first time, in *The Highlanders* (1966–1967).

16 APR 1966 *The Celestial Toymaker: The Dancing Floor*

16 APR 2005 *Aliens of London*

'You've been gone a whole year'

At the start of *Aliens of London*, the TARDIS materialises in the Powell Estate, which is Rose Tyler's home.

Rose left in the TARDIS at the end of *Rose* (2005), and since then has been to the future to see the end of the world and gone back in time to meet Charles Dickens. For viewers watching, she arrives home three weeks after we saw her run into the TARDIS. But for all that's happened to Rose while she's been away, the Ninth Doctor assures her that, as far as her family and friends will be concerned, she's been away 'about 12 hours'. Then he corrects himself. 'It's not 12 hours, it's 12 months. You've been gone a whole year – sorry.'

This shock twist means that the events of *Aliens of London* (2005) take place 12 months after the events of *Rose*. A poster seen in *Aliens of London*, appealing for information about the missing Rose, says she disappeared on 6 March 2005. That seems to give us a date for the evening she left in the TARDIS, meaning that the opening of *Rose*, and Rose's first meeting with the Doctor, takes place the previous day on 5 March.*

A scene in *The End of Time* 2 (2010) confirms that Rose first meets the Ninth Doctor in 2005, as per the missing person poster. And that surely means that the events of *Aliens of London* take place in 2006. The episode is set in the future.

The knock-on effect of this is that Rose's subsequent visits to 'contemporary' Earth in *Boom Town* and *The Parting of the Ways* (both 2005) also take place in 2006, and that *The Christmas Invasion* (2005) takes place over 24 and 25 December of that year.

That means 'contemporary' events seen in Series 2, broadcast in 2006, take place in 2007. In *The Runaway Bride* (2006), Donna Noble meets the Tenth Doctor for the first time on 24 December 2007 – a year after the events of *The Christmas Invasion,* as stated on screen.

'Contemporary' events in Series 3, broadcast in 2007, take place in 2008 and in *Voyage of the Damned* (2007), Wilfred Mott meets the Tenth Doctor for the first time on 24 December 2008. Wilf refers

---

* We've based our deductions on what we see and hear on screen. However, in *The End of the World* (2005), Rose calls her mum from the future, and Jackie tells her it is 'Wednesday'. According to the script and other sources, for Jackie this scene takes place on the same day as the early part of the episode *Rose* – that is, on the same day Rose meets the Doctor. In that case, she meets the Doctor on Wednesday 2 March 2005, leaves in the TARDIS with him on the evening of Thursday 3 March but isn't formally listed as missing until Sunday 6 March, which is the date then used on posters.

to the events of *The Runaway Bride* as 'last Christmas' and the events of *The Christmas Invasion* as 'Christmas before last'.

With one exception, 'contemporary' events in Series 4, broadcast in 2008, take place in 2009. The last of these, *Journey's End*, was broadcast on 5 July 2008, and takes place during 2009.

The next Christmas special, *The Next Doctor* (2008), is set in 1851 and not the 'present' day. The following episode, *Planet of the Dead*, was first broadcast on Easter Saturday, 11 August 2009, and also set at Easter in the 'present day' – but with no indication as to whether it's the Easter weekend of broadcast or set a year in the future.

The 2009 Christmas special, *The End of Time* 1 is once more set at Christmas in the 'present'. It includes a Christmas Day broadcast by US President Barack Obama, who, has 'promised to end the recession', implying that events here take place in 2009, not 12 months later. So Gallifrey returns on 25 December 2009. When Wilf says Donna and her fiancé Shaun Temple are 'getting married in the spring', he means 2010, about a year after Donna leaves the TARDIS.

But does that seem right given the age of Donna and Shaun's daughter Rose in *The Star Beast* and *The Giggle*, episodes explicitly set in 2023? Perhaps Donna's timeline has changed in ways we've yet to discover...

16 APR 2025 Lyrids

This is one of the oldest-known meteor showers, with recorded sightings by Chinese astronomers in 687 BCE. At their peak on the night of 22–23 April, there can be up to 18 meteors per hour. The meteors are produced by the trail of debris from comet C/1861 G1 Thatcher.

17 APR 1965 *The Crusade: The Warlords*

17 APR 1971 *Colony in Space* 2

17 APR 2010 *Victory of the Daleks*

17 APR 2022 *Legend of the Sea Devils*

17 APR 2025 Lyrids

18 APR 1964 *The Keys of Marinus: The Velvet Web*

18 APR 1970 *The Ambassadors of Death* 5

Tides on Mars

In this episode, the Third Doctor sets off into space to recover the missing crew of Mars Probe 7.

Mars is known as the 'red planet' because of the orange-red iron oxide dust that covers its surface, which can blow about in huge sandstorms. Earth scientists have studied how these 'dust tides' transport heat quickly over the planet's surface and enable currents of moisture in the air – a complex system of Martian weather.

Mars doesn't have seas because the atmospheric pressure is too low to support liquid water. But it does have polar ice caps composed largely of water. This is the native environment of a Martian culture the Doctor has encountered several times, initially in *The Ice Warriors* (1967).

Some estimates suggest that, were the atmospheric pressure to change, there's enough water in just the southern polar ice cap to flood the whole of Mars in an ocean 11 metres deep. This would surely be of interest to the viral species known as the Flood, which thrived in water, as seen in *The Waters of Mars* (2009).

What would the tides be like on this oceanic Mars? Mars has two small and irregularly shaped moons, Phobos and Deimos. But they're so small, they're likely to have less impact than the Moon does on the tides on Earth.

The fact Mars is less massive than Earth suggests that, like Venus, the waves of any Martian ocean would be slower and higher than those seen on Earth. The Flood takes people over very quickly once they have been infected by contact with contaminated water, but it might take time for that water to reach its victims.

Even so, 'water is patient,' the Doctor warns Adelaide Brooke. 'It wears down the clifftops, the mountains, the whole of the world. Water always wins.'

18 APR 1971 David John McDonald, now David Tennant, who plays the Tenth Doctor and the Fourteenth Doctor

18 APR 2025 Lyrids

19 APR 1969 *The War Games* 1

19 APR 1975 *Revenge of the Cybermen* 1

19 APR 2008 *Planet of the Ood*

19 APR 2025 Lyrids; Eta Aquarids

Earth can be moving through the trails of more than one comet at once. Overlapping with the Lyrid meteor shower, the Eta Aquarids are produced by the trail of debris from the famous Halley's comet, which featured in *Attack of the Cybermen* (1985); the same comet is also responsible for the Orionids (see 2 October). This shower is best seen from the southern hemisphere of Earth, where at peak there can be 60 meteors an hour – one every minute! From the northern hemisphere, the peak rate is about half that. This year, the peak is over the night of 6–7 May.

Lyrid and Eta Aquaria meteors can appear in any part of the sky, so how do you tell which is which? The trick is not where they *appear* but the point in the sky from which they seem to *originate*. Lyrids appear to radiate from the constellation Lyra and Eta Aquarids from near the star designated Eta Aquarii in the constellation Aquarius. It may help to use a stargazing app to locate these!

20 APR 1968 *Fury from the Deep* 6

Victoria Waterfield leaves the TARDIS

20 APR 1974 *The Monster of Peladon* 5

20 APR 2013 *Hide*

20 APR 2025 Lyrids; Eta Aquarids

20 APR 2025 Moveable Feast-er

'I don't often do Easter,' says the Tenth Doctor in *Planet of the Dead* (2009). 'I can never find it. It's always at a different time.'

Easter is a Christian festival (with a basis in earlier traditions) celebrated each spring. But the date of Easter in any year changes. The date is worked out using *computus*, the name given to the calculation. ('Calculate' and 'compute' are both words meaning 'working out', and people and devices that can work stuff out are called 'calculators' or 'computers'.) The *computus* for Easter goes like this:

- **Easter = the first Sunday after the first Full Moon after the vernal equinox**

  In fact, the vernal equinox (the point in March when we get equal amounts of daylight and night) can vary a bit each year – in 2025 it's on 20 March. That variation would make things a bit more complicated to work out, so the modern calculation of the date of Easter is:

- **Easter = the first Sunday after the first Full Moon after 21 March**

  Simple! Only, then it gets more complicated. Different Christian groups use different calendars to make the calculation. For example, the Catholic and Protestant Churches use the Gregorian calendar and the Eastern Orthodox Church uses the Julian calendar. (For more, see Making time, page 130.)

The result is that different people can calculate different dates for Easter; it depends where you are in the world, and in which culture. And how badly you want to eat your chocolate egg!

YEAR	FULL MOON	GREGORIAN EASTER	JULIAN EASTER
2020	08 APR	12 APR	19 APR
2021	28 MAR	04 APR	02 MAY
2022	16 APR	17 APR	24 APR
2023	06 APR	09 APR	16 APR
2024	25 MAR	31 MAR	05 MAY
2025	13 APR	20 APR	20 APR
2026	03 APR	05 APR	12 APR
2027	22 MAR	28 MAR	02 MAY
2028	09 APR	16 APR	16 APR
2029	29 MAR	01 APR	08 APR
2030	17 APR	21 APR	28 APR

21 APR 1973 *Planet of the Daleks* 3

21 APR 2007 *Daleks in Manhattan*

21 APR 2025 Third Quarter

One of the best mornings of the year to view the planet Mercury as it reaches 'greatest western elongation', or its highest point above the horizon in the dawn sky. Look out for a relatively bright star low in the eastern sky just before sunrise.

Lyrids

22 APR 1967 *The Faceless Ones* 3

22 APR 1972 *The Mutants* 3

22 APR 2006 *Tooth and Claw*

22 APR 2011 River Song kills the Eleventh Doctor and prevents him regenerating on the shore of Lake Silencio in Utah, in what becomes a fixed point of history and cannot possibly be changed. See *The Impossible Astronaut* (broadcast the day after this) and *The Wedding of River Song* (2011).

22 APR 2017 *Smile*

22 APR 2025 Eta Aquarids; Lyrids – peak this evening (and tomorrow morning), with about 18 meteors per hour. Given the relatively thin waning Moon, which won't cast too much light, this shower should be particularly vivid, especially on a clear night and seen from a dark location.

23 APR 1966 *The Celestial Toymaker: The Final Test*

23 APR 2005 *World War Three*

23 APR 2011 *The Impossible Astronaut*

23 APR 2016 online mini-episode *Friend from the Future*

First appearance of canteen worker Bill Potts, who travels with the Twelfth Doctor

23 APR 2025 Eta Aquarids; Lyrids – peak this morning (and last night), with about 18 meteors per hour

24 APR 1965 *The Space Museum*

24 APR 1971 *Colony in Space* 3

24 APR 2010 *The Time of Angels*

24 APR 2025 Lyrids; Eta Aquarids

25 APR 1964 *The Keys of Marinus: The Screaming Jungle*

25 APR 1970 *The Ambassadors of Death* 6

25 APR 2025 Eta Aquarids

26 APR 1969 *The War Games* 2

26 APR 1975 *Revenge of the Cybermen* 2

26 APR 2009 *The Sontaran Stratagem*

26 APR 2025 Eta Aquarids

27 APR 1968 *The Wheel in Space* 1

27 APR 1974 *The Monster of Peladon* 6

27 APR 1986 Jenna-Louise (later Jenna) Coleman, who plays the Doctor's friend Clara Oswald (and several variants of her).

27 APR 2013 *Journey to the Centre of the TARDIS*

27 APR 2025 New Moon

Eta Aquarids

28 APR 1973 *Planet of the Daleks* 4

28 APR 2007 *Evolution of the Daleks*

28 APR 2025 Eta Aquarids

29 APR 1967 *The Faceless Ones* 4

29 APR 1972 *The Mutants* 4

29 APR 2006 *School Reunion*

29 APR 2017 *Thin Ice*

Record of achievement

To coincide with this, the 819th regular episode of *Doctor Who*, Guinness World Records named the series the 'Most prolific science-fiction TV series (by episode)'. But the broadcast of *Thin Ice* didn't see *Doctor Who* overtake some previous record-holding TV show that had run for 818 episodes; the reasoning behind the new record seems to have been a bit more complicated.

First, *Doctor Who* had held Guinness World Records before. In 2001, it was recognised as being 'the largest fictional series built around one principal character'. But this was in the midst of the 16-year period when *Doctor Who* was not being made on TV (bar one TV movie); the record instead acknowledged the prolific range of *Doctor Who* novels.

In 2007, Guinness World Records recognised *Doctor Who*, now back on TV, as the 'longest running science-fiction series in the world'. Two years later, Guinness World Records went further and recognised *Doctor Who* as 'the most successful sci-fi series', based on more than just the number of episodes or years it had run. Ratings, sales of merchandise and other factors were also considered.

That's a fine accolade and something to be proud of. But compare the success of *Doctor Who* to other long-running series such as *Star Trek*, which by 2017 comprised multiple different TV incarnations – *Star Trek* (1966–1969), *The Next Generation* (1987–1994), *Deep Space Nine* (1993–1999), *Voyager* (1995–2001) and *Enterprise* (2001–2005) – as well as movies, an animated TV series and a wealth of merchandise. The *Doctor Who* episode *Thin Ice* was broadcast a few months ahead of the launch of a seventh *Star Trek* TV series: *Discovery* (2017–2024). This has since been followed by *Picard* (2020–2023) and *Strange New Worlds* (2022–), as well as more animated series and the promise of further movies. Doesn't that compete with the success of *Doctor Who*?

The distinction seems to be that these new incarnations are separate TV series under the umbrella title *Star Trek*, whereas *Thin Ice* is the 819th episode of a single TV series running since 1963. Oh, and not all episodes of *Doctor Who* are counted in this total.

Guinness World Records does not include the 1996 TV movie or other feature-length episodes such as Christmas specials in its count. Including those, *Thin Ice* is the 830th episode of *Doctor Who*. And though the Guinness World Records website still lists

Doctor Who as 'Most prolific science-fiction TV series (by episode)', based on the 819 regular episodes up to and including *Thin Ice*, there has of course been much more *Doctor Who* since then. Including specials, the most recent episode to date, *Empire of Death*, is number 883.

29 APR 2025 Eta Aquarids

30 APR ANNUALLY Beltane is 'the greatest occult festival of the year', according to white witch Miss Olive Hawthorne in *The Dæmons* (1971).

30 APR 1966 *The Gunfighters: A Holiday for the Doctor*

30 APR 2005 *Dalek*

30 APR 2011 *Day of the Moon*

30 APR 2025 Eta Aquarids

♥♥+
MAY

01 MAY 1965 *The Space Museum: The Dimensions of Time*

01 MAY 1971 *Colony in Space* 4

01 MAY 197?/198? UNIT soldiers arrest the Master in the village of Devil's End, *The Dæmons* (1971)

UNIT dating
The Doctor isn't sure when his time as scientific adviser to UNIT takes place – *Pyramids of Mars* (1975) implies it is in 1980; *Mawdryn Undead* (1983) suggests he had left his post by 1977. Time's in flux.

01 MAY 1984 Traditional May Day crowning of the May Queen takes a sinister turn due to psychic aliens' influence in *The Awakening* (1984)

01 MAY 2010 *Flesh and Stone*

01 MAY 2025 Eta Aquarids

02 MAY 1964 *The Keys of Marinus: The Snows of Terror*

02 MAY 1970 *The Ambassadors of Death* 7

02 MAY 2025 Eta Aquarids

03 MAY 1969 *The War Games* 3

03 MAY 1975 *Revenge of the Cybermen* 3

03 MAY 2008 *The Poison Sky*

03 MAY 2025 Eta Aquarids

📅 **04 MAY 1699** Lemuel Gulliver sets sail from Bristol at the start of the classic satirical novel *Gulliver's Travels* (1726), but being an entirely fictional character doesn't prevent him from meeting the Second Doctor in *The Mind Robber* (1968).

📺 **04 MAY 1968** *The Wheel in Space* 2

1st First appearance of space librarian Zoe Heriot, who travels with the Second Doctor

📺 **04 MAY 1974** *Planet of the Spiders* 1

04 MAY 2013 *The Crimson Horror*

🌓 **04 MAY 2025** First Quarter

☄ Eta Aquarids

📺 **05 MAY 1973** *Planet of the Daleks* 5

05 MAY 2007 *The Lazarus Experiment*

☄ **05 MAY 2025** Eta Aquarids

📺 **06 MAY 1967** *The Faceless Ones* 5

06 MAY 1972 *The Mutants* 5

06 MAY 2006 *The Girl in the Fireplace*

06 MAY 2017 *Knock Knock*

The title of this episode is surely a reference to the old joke:

Knock knock
Who's there?
Doctor
Doctor who?

Jokes are good. They can brighten up your day. Research suggests that humour can also lower stress, enhance your mood, brain power and energy levels, and perhaps even improve your immunity to disease. No joke, seriously!

But this knock-knock gag is *such* an old joke. Surely there are new jokes related to the Doctor. And surely you can do better than these:

What does Davros eat with pizza?
Dalek bread.

Where do Cybermen wipe their feet?
On the Cybermats.

What's obtuse and can send you back in time?
A Weeping Angle.

Which Australian animal travels in the TARDIS?
A kanga-ruby.

06 MAY 2025 Eta Aquarids – peak

07 MAY 1895 First publication of the science-fiction novel *The Time Machine* by Herbert George Wells, partly inspired by his adventures ten years earlier with the Sixth Doctor and Peri on the planet Karfel, in *Timelash* (1985).

In fact, in 1963 BBC head of drama Sydney Newman drew inspiration from *The Time Machine* (and many other sources) when conceiving his idea for a new TV series, *Doctor Who*.

07 MAY 1966 *The Gunfighters: Don't Shoot the Pianist*

07 MAY 2005 *The Long Game*

07 MAY 2011 *The Curse of the Black Spot*

See the entry on Canis Major (page 41) for more about the star Sirius mentioned in this episode.

07 MAY 2025 Eta Aquarids – peak

08 MAY 1813 The Fifteenth Doctor and Ruby Sunday attend a ball, as seen in *Rogue* (2024).

08 MAY 1965 *The Space Museum: The Search*

08 MAY 1971 *Colony in Space* 5

08 MAY 2010 *The Vampires of Venice*

08 MAY 2025 Eta Aquarids

We've seen before how the Moon affects the tides on Earth and how the Sun might affect oceans on Venus and Mars (if there were any). But what about when the bodies involved are of more equal size – such as four moons or twin planets?

Earth and Venus are sometimes referred to as 'twin planets' because they're both about the same size and mass. Venus is also our closest neighbour in the Solar System. But our twin has no noticeable direct impact on Earth.

In contrast, when the Fifth Doctor and Peri visit the planet Androzani Minor (in *The Caves of Androzani* (1984)), they discover that its twin planet Androzani Major has a dramatic impact. As the Doctor explains, the core of Androzani Minor is composed of 'superheated primeval mud'. When the planet's orbit takes it close to its twin, the larger planet's mavitational force acts on the mud in the same way that our Sun and Moon affect Earth's oceans.

The result, says Peri, is 'mud baths for everyone', a deadly danger to anyone on the planet's surface or in its caves underground. Even so, the explosions of mud aren't random events. Because they're linked to the orbits of the two planets, they can be predicted. In fact, they are tidal.

Indeed, exploring this world for the first time, the Doctor and Peri both refer to tides because what they see of the landscape reminds them of the effects of the sea on the landscape on Earth.

We know this kind of 'tidal' effect on the insides of an orbiting body is going on in our own neighbourhood of space. Jupiter, the largest and most massive planet in our Solar System, has a similar impact on several of its moons. That's especially evident on Io, a moon slightly larger than our own.

Io is caught in a mavitational tug-of-war between Jupiter and its other three large moons – Europa, Ganymede and Callisto.

Getting pulled around in the intense mavity close to its giant parent planet creates tidal heating inside Io that makes it the most geologically active place in the Solar System, with more than 400 active volcanoes.

Io's surface is dusted with a yellow frost of sulphur dioxide which rains down from these volcanoes, smoothing out surface features. That smooth, yellowish surface means that, seen from space, the disc of Io resembles a cheesy pizza.

Europa and Ganymede are also affected by tidal flexing, though not quite to the dramatic degree seen on Io. They're a dynamic, volatile family.

09 MAY 1964 *The Keys of Marinus: Sentence of Death*

09 MAY 1970 *Inferno* 1

09 MAY 2025 Eta Aquarids

10 MAY 1969 *The War Games* 4

10 MAY 1975 *Revenge of the Cybermen* 4

10 MAY 2008 *The Doctor's Daughter*

10 MAY 2024 *Space Babies* and *The Devil's Chord* on Disney+ in some time zones

Slightly ahead

'I have the advantage of being slightly ahead of you,' says the Fourth Doctor in *Pyramids of Mars* (1975). 'Sometimes behind you but normally ahead of you.'

The same thing is true of UK broadcasts of new episodes of *Doctor Who*, which usually take place ahead of anywhere else in the world. But, on occasion, the UK is behind other countries, such as when *The Five Doctors* (1983) and the TV movie (1996) were shown in the USA a few days ahead of the UK.

The 2024 series of *Doctor Who* has seen something new – and at first sight rather odd. New episodes were broadcast on TV in the UK in what has often been the usual transmission slot: early on Saturday evenings. But the episodes were also released on BBC iPlayer earlier on the same day, at midnight, and made available around the world on Disney+ at exactly the same time.

The Earth is turning on its axis every 24 hours (in a period we call a 'day'). That means when one side of the Earth is facing the sun (in 'daytime'), the other side of Earth is in shadow (or 'night'). The time of any given day is therefore relative to your position on the Earth's surface, and when it is midnight in the UK, in the USA it is still early evening on the previous day.

The result is that the first new episodes of the 2024 series were released in the UK on 11 May and in the US on 10 May – but were released at exactly the same time. A timey-wimey paradox that's very apt for the Doctor!

10 MAY 2025 Eta Aquarids

11 MAY 1968 *The Wheel in Space* 3

11 MAY 1974 *Planet of the Spiders* 2

11 MAY 2013 *Nightmare in Silver*

11 MAY 2024 *Space Babies* and *The Devil's Chord* in the UK

11 MAY 2025 Eta Aquarids

12 MAY 1973 *Planet of the Daleks* 6

12 MAY 1996 *Doctor Who* (TV movie), on Canadian television

First appearance of the Eighth Doctor, who also claims to be 'half human, on my mother's side', the first time this aspect of the Doctor's history has been mentioned; first appearance of a new incarnation of the Master

12 MAY 1999 Pioneering astronaut Adelaide Brooke born in Finchley, London, according to *The Waters of Mars* (2009)

12 MAY 2025 Full Moon

Eta Aquarids

13 MAY 1967 *The Faceless Ones* 6

Ben Jackson and Polly leave the TARDIS

13 MAY 1972 *The Mutants* 6

13 MAY 1985 Psychic time traveller Claire Brown born, though when living in 1967 she says she was born on the same date in 1935. See *Village of the Angels* (2021).

13 MAY 2006 *Rise of the Cybermen*

🚪 The Daleks first used their catchphrase 'Exterminate!' in 1964, a year after their first appearance. The Cybermen had to wait almost 40 years for a catchphrase of their own. Having first appeared on screen in 1966, they first utter 'Delete!' in this episode.

📺 **13 MAY 2017** *Oxygen*

☄️ **13 MAY 2025** Eta Aquarids

📺 **14 MAY 1966** *The Gunfighters: Johnny Ringo*

14 MAY 1996 *Doctor Who* (TV movie) in the US

14 MAY 2005 *Father's Day*

14 MAY 2011 *The Doctor's Wife*

☄️ **14 MAY 2025** Eta Aquarids

🚪📅 **15 MAY 1963** The earliest recorded reference to *Doctor Who*, on a draft document of notes on the background and approach to be taken with the series, typed by BBC secretary Margaret Turner on behalf of head of serials Donald Wilson. (An earlier memo, dated 9 May, refers to *Mr Who?* Even though that's wrong, it suggests the title had already been agreed by this point!)

THE ~~MACHINE~~ *Ship*

Dr. Who has a "machine" which enables them to travel together through space, through time, and through matter. When first seen, this machine has the appearance of a police box standing in the street, but anyone entering it is immediately inside an extensive electronic contrivance.

Though it looks impressive, it is an old beat-up model which Dr. Who stole when he escaped from his own galaxy in the year 5733; it is uncertain in performance ~~and often needs repairing~~ *isn't quite certain*; moreover, Dr. Who has ~~forgott~~en how to work it, so they have to learn by trial and error.

A revised document dated the following day adds a little further detail, such as that the 'shabby' police box exterior 'conceals a vast chromium and glass interior of a kind of spaceship'.

Something special had begun...

15 MAY 1965 *The Space Museum: The Final Phase*

15 MAY 1971 *Colony in Space* 6

15 MAY 2010 *Amy's Choice*

15 MAY 2025 Eta Aquarids

This month's constellation: Boötes

Last month, we identified the easy-to-find constellation Ursa Major (see page 67). This month, we're going to use that constellation to help us find another that is somewhat harder to spot.

Follow the direction of the curved tail of the bear and you can 'arc' to Arcturus, the brightest star in the constellation Boötes and the third brightest star in the night sky. Arcturus is slightly orange in colour – which you may be able to see with the naked eye but is more evident when seen through binoculars.

This is the home of the unnamed delegate from Arcturus seen in *The Curse of Peladon* (1972),[*] whom the Doctor refers to as 'Arcturus', which would be like calling you 'Earth'.

---

[*] The same story introduces a character called Alpha Centauri, presumably from the relatively bright triple star system in the (real) constellation of Centaurus. That star system includes Proxima Centauri – the closest star to our own Sun.

Boötes is a kite-shaped constellation, said to look like a 'herdsman' out hunting. Meteors can appear anywhere in the night sky, but we can identify Quadrantid meteors because they seem to radiate from a point within this constellation. See 1 January 2025 for tips on spotting meteors.

16 MAY 1964 *The Keys of Marinus*

16 MAY 1970 *Inferno* 2

16 MAY 2025 Eta Aquarids

17 MAY 1900 'Relief of Mafeking', ending a 217-day siege of a town now known as Mahikeng in South Africa during the Second Boer War; the Doctor was there, according to *The Daleks' Master Plan* (1965–1966).

In November 1913, schoolmaster John Smith (a human form of the Tenth Doctor) intends to lend pupil Timothy Latimer a definitive account of the events at Mafeking written by an 'Aitchison Price', in *Human Nature* (2007).

17 MAY 1969 *The War Games* 5

17 MAY 2008 *The Unicorn and the Wasp*

What to feed a poisoned Doctor

The Tenth Doctor, Donna and Agatha Christie team up to solve a particularly strange murder mystery. But the culprit tries to cover their tracks – by murdering the Doctor. A deadly poison called cyanide is slipped into his drink and the Doctor gulps it down.

Agatha says there's no cure for cyanide, but the Doctor isn't human and can stimulate his inhibited enzymes to detoxify the poison. For this he needs:

- Ginger beer (as found in pantries)
- Protein (as found in walnuts)
- Salt (as found in anchovies)
- A shock (as found in Donna kissing him)

17 MAY 2024 *Boom* on Disney+ in some time zones

🍴 Bananas are good

This episode isn't the first to mention the weapon factories of Villengard. We learn in *The Doctor Dances* (2005) that the factories were vaporised in the 51st century after the Doctor made the reactors go critical. 'There's a banana grove there, now,' says the Ninth Doctor. 'I like bananas. Bananas are good.'

Bananas are a good source of potassium, which can help to regulate the workings of your heart. They're also high in fibre and help to neutralise stomach acid and heart burn. They can make you feel good, too, because they contain amino acid tryptophan, which your body converts into serotonin – the brain chemical that makes you happier.

The potassium in bananas is very slightly radioactive. This isn't enough to be harmful, but an average banana produces about 15 positrons a second. Positrons are tiny, subatomic particles just like ordinary electrons but with a positive rather than negative electrical charge. Another name for equal-but-opposite particles such as positrons is 'antimatter'. There's a spaceship powered by antimatter in *Earthshock* (1982) and a whole world made from the stuff plus Omega's mental energy in *The Three Doctors* (1972–1973). Someone has clearly been eating a lot of bananas!

Oh, and if you want to make someone else feel good, you can make a banana look exactly like a penguin.

1. Grasp the stalk and yank it back from the outer curve of the banana, opening the skin
2. The idea is to peel back a section about one-third of the circumference of the skin, leaving two-thirds round the inner-curve of the banana
3. Now split that two-thirds section down the middle of the inner curve, creating two wings
4. Flip the stalk back on to the top of the banana to create the head and beak

1.

2.

3.

4.

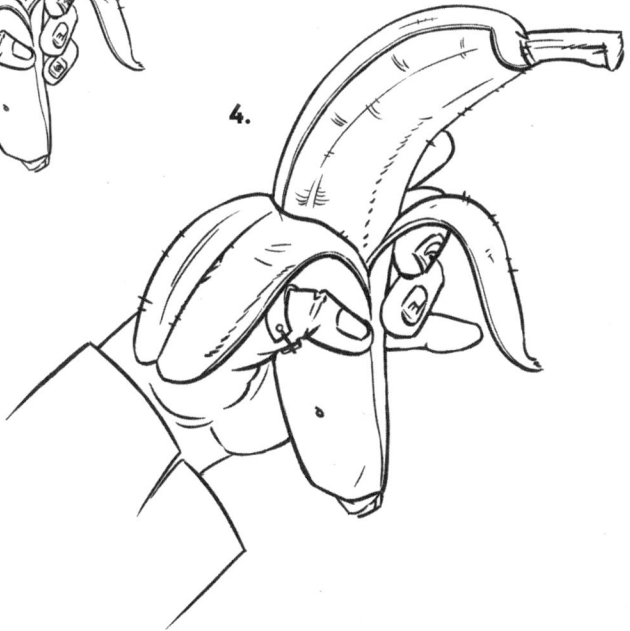

17 MAY 2025 Eta Aquarids

18 MAY 1968 *The Wheel in Space* 4

18 MAY 1974 *Planet of the Spiders* 3

18 MAY 2013 *The Name of the Doctor*

First appearance of the War Doctor

18 MAY 2024 *Boom*

18 MAY 2025 Eta Aquarids

19 MAY 1973 *The Green Death* 1

Jo Grant leaves the TARDIS.

19 MAY 2007 *42*

19 MAY 2025 Eta Aquarids

20 MAY 1967 *The Evil of the Daleks* 1

20 MAY 1972 *The Time Monster* 1

20 MAY 2006 *The Age of Steel*

20 MAY 2017 *Extremis*

20 MAY 2025 Third Quarter

Eta Aquarids

21 MAY 1966 *The Gunfighters: The OK Corral*

21 MAY 2005 *The Empty Child*

First appearance of rogue time agent calling himself 'Captain Jack Harkness', who travels with the Ninth, Tenth and Thirteenth Doctors

21 MAY 2011 *The Rebel Flesh*

21 MAY 2025 Eta Aquarids

22 MAY 1965 *The Chase: The Executioners*

22 MAY 1971 *The Dæmons* 1

22 MAY 2010 *The Hungry Earth*

22 MAY 2025 Eta Aquarids

23 MAY 1964 *The Aztecs: The Temple of Evil*

23 MAY 1970 *Inferno* 3

23 MAY 2025 Eta Aquarids

24 MAY 1969 *The War Games* 6

First mention of the Time Lords

24 MAY 2024 *73 Yards* on Disney+ in some time zones

24 MAY 2025 Eta Aquarids (see 19 April 2025)

25 MAY 1969 *The Wheel in Space* 5

25 MAY 1974 *Planet of the Spiders* 4

25 MAY 2024 *73 Yards*

25 MAY 2025 Eta Aquarids

26 MAY 1973 *The Green Death* 2

26 MAY 2007 *Human Nature*

26 MAY 2025 Eta Aquarids

27 MAY 1967 *The Evil of the Daleks* 2

First appearance of Victoria Waterfield, who travels with the Second Doctor

27 MAY 1972 *The Time Monster* 2

27 MAY 1996 *Doctor Who* (TV movie) in UK

27 MAY 2006 *The Idiot's Lantern*

27 MAY 2017 *The Pyramid at the End of the World*

27 MAY 2025 New Moon

Eta Aquarids

28 MAY 1966 *The Savages* 1

28 MAY 2005 *The Doctor Dances*

28 MAY 2011 *The Almost People*

28 MAY 2025 Eta Aquarids

29 MAY 1965 *The Chase: The Death of Time*

29 MAY 1971 *The Dæmons* 2

29 MAY 1987 Pearl Mackie, who plays the Doctor's friend Bill Potts

29 MAY 2010 *Cold Blood*

30 MAY 1964 *The Aztecs: The Warriors of Death*

30 MAY 1970 *Inferno* 4

31 MAY 1969 *The War Games* 7

31 MAY 2008 *Silence in the Library*

First appearance of archaeologist Professor River Song, who travels with the Eleventh and Twelfth Doctors

31 MAY 2024 *Dot and Bubble* on Disney+ in some time zones

31 MAY 2025 This is a good morning to view planet Venus as it reaches its highest point above the horizon (or 'greatest western elongation'). It looks like a relatively large, bright star in the eastern sky just before sunrise.

♥♥+
JUNE

01 JUN 1890 The Eleventh Doctor and Amy Pond meet the artist Vincent van Gogh and stay with him over the next two days, battling a giant invisible alien creature in *Vincent and the Doctor* (2010).

01 JUN 1968 *The Wheel in Space 6*

01 JUN 1974 *Planet of the Spiders 5*

01 JUN 2024 *Dot and Bubble*

02 JUN 1866 The Second Doctor and Jamie McCrimmon find themselves transported back in time a hundred years from London on 20 July 1966 to Professor Maxtible's house a few miles from Canterbury, where some old enemies await in *The Evil of the Daleks* (1967).

02 JUN 1890 Events of *Vincent and the Doctor* (2010)

02 JUN 1953 Coronation of Queen Elizabeth II, the longest reigning British monarch and second longest reigning monarch in the world. More than 20 million people in the UK watched the Coronation live on television that particular Tuesday. An alien entity called the Wire sought to feed on this audience in *The Idiot's Lantern* (2006).

02 JUN 1973 *The Green Death 3*

02 JUN 2007 *The Family of Blood*

03 JUN 1890 Events of *Vincent and the Doctor* (2010)

📺 **03 JUN 1967** *The Evil of the Daleks* 3

03 JUN 1972 *The Time Monster* 3

03 JUN 2006 *The Impossible Planet*

03 JUN 2017 *The Lie of the Land*

🌓 **03 JUN 2025** First Quarter

📅 **04 JUN 1926** The Third Doctor and Jo Grant arrive on the SS *Bernice* sailing across the Indian Ocean and bound for Bombay, though things aren't quite what they seem in *Carnival of Monsters* (1973).

🌊 Tides in a Miniscope

The Third Doctor has heard of the SS *Bernice*, which he says disappeared at sea two days out from Bombay. 'A freak tidal wave was the popular explanation,' he says, 'although the Indian Ocean was as flat as a millpond on that night.'

In fact, we can check the phase of the Moon for that night to see whether the ocean was subject to tidal forces. Friday 4 June 1926 was almost exactly halfway between a Full Moon and New Moon, when Earth, Sun and Moon are aligned. Those nights are when combined mavitational forces make for the biggest tides, so there's evidence to support the popular explanation.

Yet, as the Doctor and Jo soon discover, something much stranger is going on. The SS *Bernice* has been captured, miniaturised and made a kind of specimen inside a machine. The machine preserves the ship, its passengers and crew, and holds them in a time loop. They're unaware they've been captured, not noticing that it's always the same day. And they're always surprised when, exactly on schedule, the same plesiosaur attacks them.

We don't know how large this specimen is within the Miniscope machine, but there must be enough sea included for the plesiosaur to explore, so that it doesn't attack the SS *Bernice* all the time and the passengers don't spot it before it strikes. Some of the other environments we see within the Miniscope are very big indeed – the Doctor and Jo later encounter enormous Drashigs while out in a vast landscape. So the section of sea on which the SS *Bernice* floats could be very big indeed.

Yet the sense is that this sea remains eerily calm and unchanging. Given the close proximity of other massive environments, the Miniscope must have the ability to cancel out tidal forces. There are no tides inside the machine.

04 JUN 1966 *The Savages* 2

04 JUN 2005 *Boom Town*

04 JUN 2011 *A Good Man Goes to War*

First appearances of Silurian Madame Vastra, her human wife Jenny Flint and their Sontaran servant Strax

05 JUN 1965 *The Chase: Flight Through Eternity*

05 JUN 1971 *The Dæmons* 3

05 JUN 1994 Clyde Langer, who, through his friend Sarah Jane Smith, met both the Tenth and Eleventh Doctors; his date of birth given in *The Sarah Jane Adventures: Secrets of the Stars* (2008).

05 JUN 2010 *Vincent and the Doctor*

06 JUN 1964 *The Aztecs: The Bride of Sacrifice*

06 JUN 1970 *Inferno* 5

07 JUN 1969 *The War Games* 8

07 JUN 1977 Silver Jubilee celebrations marking 25 years since the ascension to the throne of Queen Elizabeth II; on this day, the Doctor's friend the Brigadier loses his memory. See *Mawdryn Undead* (1983).

07 JUN 2008 *Forest of the Dead*

7 JUN 2024 *Rogue* on Disney+ in some time zones

08 JUN 1943 Colin Baker, who plays the Sixth Doctor (and also Maxil in *Arc of Infinity* (1983))

08 JUN 1974 *Planet of the Spiders* 6

First appearance of the Fourth Doctor

08 JUN 2024 *Rogue*

09 JUN 1973 *The Green Death* 4

09 JUN 2007 *Blink*

10 JUN 1967 *The Evil of the Daleks* 4

10 JUN 1972 *The Time Monsters* 4

10 JUN 2006 *The Satan Pit*

10 JUN 2017 *Empress of Mars*

11 JUN 1925 The Fifth Doctor plays very good cricket for the club at Cranleigh Halt, as seen in *Black Orchid* (1982).

11 JUN 1966 *The Savages* 3

11 JUN 2005 *Bad Wolf*

11 JUN 2025 Full Moon

12 JUN 1965 *The Chase: Journey into Terror*

12 JUN 1971 *The Dæmons* 4

12 JUN 2010 *The Lodger*

13 JUN 1964 *The Aztecs: The Day of Darkness*

13 JUN 1970 *Inferno* 6

14 JUN 1969 *The War Games* 9

14 JUN 2008 *Midnight*

14 JUN 2024 *The Legend of Ruby Sunday* on Disney+ in some time zones

15 JUN 1752 Benjamin Franklin's kite and almanac

On this night (some sources suggest it was 10 June), Benjamin Franklin and his son William flew a kite into a thunderstorm in Philadelphia, in what's now the USA. 'That was a day and a half,' says the Tenth Doctor in *Smith and Jones* (2007). 'I got rope burns off that kite and then I got soaked ... And then I got electrocuted!'

Franklin was conducting a scientific experiment. At the time, people didn't know what caused lightning or how to stop lightning strikes from damaging buildings. Franklin thought lightning had something to do with electricity and set out to prove it.

Now, as the Doctor says, this experiment was very dangerous so **don't try it yourself**. But this is what Franklin did:

The kite was specially constructed for the experiment. They used a silk handkerchief rather than paper so that it wouldn't tear in the rain. A pointed spike of wire was attached to the top of the kite to conduct electricity when lightning struck it. A string then trailed down from the kite to where Franklin (and the Doctor) held it.

Towards the bottom of this string, near the hand holding it, they fastened a piece of silk ribbon and a metal key. Franklin said care had to be taken to keep this ribbon under cover so it did not get wet, while at the same time ensuring that the kite string did not touch whatever cover they used. It's thought this precaution may have helped ensure he did not receive a deadly electrical shock.

With all this prepared, Franklin (and the Doctor) flew the kite during a thunderstorm – and it didn't get struck by lightning.

And yet, just flying it into the thunderclouds produced the most extraordinary effect. Franklin saw the tiny fibres of the kite string standing up in all directions. When he moved his fingers close, the fibres were attracted. More dramatically, when he moved his finger towards the metal key, he received a small electrical shock.

Franklin (and the Doctor) also seem to have run a wire from the key down to a special kind of glass bottle that had only recently been invented to store high-voltage electric charge. They used this 'Leyden jar' (the name taken from the Dutch city of Leiden, the home of one of the scientists working on this stuff) to collect electrical charge from lightning, conducted down through the kite from the clouds.

From this successful experiment, Franklin came up with a brilliant invention. In September 1852, he attached a metal rod to his house that, should it be struck by lightning, would conduct away the electrical charge without damage to the building. The following month, Franklin shared details of this invention in the latest edition of his popular book, *Poor Richard's Almanac* – encouraging people all over the country and abroad to try it for themselves.

The result was that buildings fitted with lightning conductors were saved from destruction in storms. Franklin's experiments and the way he shared his discoveries helped develop our understanding of electrical charges, and the way electricity could be put to practical use – so every electrical or electronic device today owes a debt to Franklin's kite.

Franklin's kite experiment changed the world in other ways, too. It helped make Franklin famous. He received an honorary degree from the prestigious Harvard University, while in London the Royal Society awarded Franklin a gold Copley medal – its highest award. Even Louis XV, King of France, sent Franklin a congratulatory letter.

This fame was partly why Franklin was later sent to both London and France on behalf of the American people. At the time, America was an English colony but there were serious complaints about the way it was run. Franklin became frustrated with the lack of response to these complaints in England and was one of the first people to suggest that the American states should form a union of their own. Franklin's relationship with the French king and queen was instrumental in getting French support for what became the American War of Independence.

In fact, the noted science-fiction writer Isaac Asimov wrote a whole non-fiction book, *The Kite that Won the Revolution* (1963), which traces the creation of the United States back to that stormy day in June 1752 when Franklin (and the Doctor) flew a kite – and changed the whole future.

15 JUN 1999 Rosa Parks awarded the Congressional Gold Medal in recognition of her being 'mother of the modern civil rights movement'. The Thirteenth Doctor, having met Rosa in the 1950s in *Rosa* (2018), explains that this is 'the highest award given to any civilian [in the USA], recognising her as a living icon for freedom'.

15 JUN 2024 *The Legend of Ruby Sunday*

This month's constellation: Virgo

Last month, we used the tail of Ursa Major to 'arc' to Arcturus (see page 91). Keep going, and you 'speed' to Spica, the brightest star in Virgo or the 'maiden', which looks a little like a stick figure of a person. This is the largest constellation in the zodiac (see page 14) and the second largest constellation in the sky.

'Spica' is the Latin word for an ear of wheat, which seems to come from a very ancient pattern seen in these stars. In the Babylonian star catalogue MUL.APIN – which was compiled in about 1,000 BCE but based on much older traditions – Spica is one of the ears of wheat growing in a furrow in the ground.

It's not the first connection we've seen between farming and the stars – see also the 'Plough' in Ursa Major (page 67). Recognisable patterns of stars – and their regular movements over the course of the year – acted a bit like a calendar, helping ancient farmers to know exactly when to sow and harvest their crops – the Sun is passing through this constellation at harvest time. Their food source, their communities, depended on recognising these stars.

Some ancient Greeks and Romans identified the figure seen in this constellation with Demeter, goddess of harvest and farming, and there's a reference to her in *The Trial of a Time Lord* (1986). In the 30th century, the agronomist Professor Sarah Lasky develops a strain of plant so hardy it can grow in desert sand, with the potential to increase crop yields by three times. Her assistant, Bruchner, names what they have created after that ancient goddess: 'Demeter seeds'.

🗓 16 JUN 1816

On holiday in a villa in Switzerland, a group of friends are stuck indoors for days because of very dark, wet weather. To entertain themselves, they read ghost stories from a book called *Fantasmagoriana* and then try to write their own unsettling tales...

The Thirteenth Doctor, Yaz, Ryan and Graham arrive just in time to witness this historic moment – when Mary Wollstonecraft Godwin (soon to be Mary Shelley) begins writing her novel *Frankenstein, or the Modern Prometheus*. It's a gruesome story, about a brilliant, immoral young scientist who puts bits of different dead bodies together and then uses electricity to bring this creature to life... First published in 1818, the thrilling, scary book quickly won praise. Today, *Frankenstein* is seen as a key work in the history of horror fiction. To many scholars, it's also the first true work of science fiction.

See *The Haunting of Villa Diodati* (2020). Frankenstein's creature appears (and battles Daleks!) in *The Chase: Journey into Terror* (1965).

16 JUN 1973 *The Green Death* 5

16 JUN 2007 *Utopia*

First appearance of a new incarnation of the Master

17 JUN 1967 *The Evil of the Daleks* 5

17 JUN 1972 *The Time Monster* 5

17 JUN 1982 Jodie Auckland Whittaker, who plays the Thirteenth Doctor

17 JUN 2006 *Love & Monsters*

17 JUN 2017 *The Eaters of Light*

18 JUN 1815 The Battle of Waterloo, fought in what's now Belgium, sees the defeat of French Emperor Napoleon Bonaparte (who appears in *The Reign of Terror* (1964)). The Tenth Doctor, in the human form of schoolmaster John Smith, teaches his pupils about the military tactics of this battle in *Human Nature* (2007).

18 JUN 1966 *The Savages* 4

Steven Taylor leaves the TARDIS

18 JUN 1988 Novelty song 'Doctorin' the TARDIS' by the Timelords (sic), later the KLF, reaches no. 1 in the UK singles charts.

This is the most successful of a number of pop songs related to *Doctor Who*, and the Timelords (aka Jimmy Cauty and Bill Drummond) even wrote a guidebook on how they'd done it, *The Manual (How to Have a Number One the Easy Way)*, published the same year.

Other examples of *Doctor Who* novelty records include 1972's 'Who Is the Doctor' sung by Third Doctor actor Jon Pertwee, 1968's 'Who's Dr Who?' sung by Frazer Hines (who played companion Jamie McCrimmon) and 1965's 'Who's Who' sung by Roberta Tovey (who played companion Susan in the two Dalek movies). The Timelords may owe their no. 1 hit to the fact that they avoided a terrible pun on the word 'Who'.

Also notable is 'Doctor?', a dance version of the *Doctor Who* theme by electronic band Orbital, included on their 2001 album *The Altogether* (and immediately followed by a track that begins with Fourth Doctor actor Tom Baker asking, 'Can't you get us out of here?'). On 27 June 2010, Orbital performed 'Doctor?' live on stage at the Glastonbury Festival, accompanied by Eleventh Doctor actor Matt Smith.

18 JUN 2005 *The Parting of the Ways*

18 JUN 2025 Third Quarter

19 JUN 1965 *The Chase: The Death of Doctor Who*

19 JUN 1971 *The Dæmons* 5

19 JUN 2004 Amelia Eve 'Millie' Gibson, who plays the Doctor's friend Ruby Sunday

19 JUN 2010 *The Pandorica Opens*

20 JUN 1964 *The Sensorites: Strangers in Space*

20 JUN 1970 *Inferno* 7

21 JUN 1969 *The War Games* 10

Jamie McCrimmon and Zoe Heriot leave the TARDIS

21 JUN 2008 *Turn Left*

21 JUN 2024 *Empire of Death* on Disney+ in some time zones

21 JUN 2025 Summer solstice: the northern hemisphere gets the longest day and the southern hemisphere the longest night. It's the effect of the Earth spinning on an axis angled 23.4° to the plane of its orbit, which means a changing amount of sunlight received over the course of the year.

22 JUN 2024 *Empire of Death*

23 JUN 1973 *The Green Death* 6

23 JUN 2007 *The Sound of Drums*

24 JUN 1967 *The Evil of the Daleks* 6

24 JUN 1972 *The Time Monsters* 6

24 JUN 2006 *Fear Her*

24 JUN 2017 *World Enough and Time*

25 JUN 1966 *The War Machines* 1

First appearance of secretary Polly and able seaman Ben Jackson, who travel with the First and Second Doctors

25 JUN 2010 Amy Pond joins the Eleventh Doctor travelling in the TARDIS in *The Eleventh Hour* (2010). That night, Rory Williams joins Amy and the Eleventh Doctor travelling in the TARDIS in *The Vampires of Venice* (2010).

25 JUN 2025 New Moon

26 JUN 1890 The discovery of a Zygon spaceship under the Savoy Hotel interrupts Amy Pond and Rory Williams' -120th wedding anniversary celebrations, in *The Power of Three* (2012).

26 JUN 1965 *The Chase: The Planet of Decision*

First appearance of space pilot Steven Taylor, who travels with the First Doctor

Barbara Wright and Ian Chesterton leave the TARDIS

26 JUN 2010 *The Big Bang*

The Silents cause the Doctor's TARDIS to explode, which destroys almost the whole universe and leaves cracks all through time and space; later that day, Amy Pond marries Rory Williams, all on the same day as broadcast.

27 JUN 1964 *The Sensorites: The Unwilling Warriors*

28 JUN 1914 Archduke Franz Ferdinand of Austria is shot and killed by Bosnian Serb activist Gavrilo Princip, which leads, 'through nations having treaties with nations, like a line of dominoes falling' – as the Tenth Doctor puts it in *The Family of Blood* (2007) – to the outbreak of the First World War.

28 JUN 2008 *The Stolen Earth*

29 JUN 1943 Maureen O'Brien, who plays the Doctor's friend Vicki

29 JUN none – See *A Holiday for the Doctor* (page 140).

30 JUN 2007 *Last of the Time Lords*

Martha Jones leaves the TARDIS

♥♥+
JULY

01 JUL 1967 *The Evil of the Daleks* 7

01 JUL 2006 *Army of Ghosts*

01 JUL 2017 *The Doctor Falls*

Bill Potts and Nardole leave the TARDIS

01 JUL 2058 Bowie Base One established in the Gusev crater, the first human settlement on planet Mars. See *The Waters of Mars* (2009).

02 JUL 1966 *The War Machines* 2

Dodo Chaplet leaves the TARDIS

02 JUL 2025 First Quarter

03 JUL 1965 *The Time Meddler: The Watcher*

03 JUL 2379 The Sixth Doctor and Peri arrive on planet Thoros-Beta, the date given by the Valeyard as '24th century, last quarter, fourth year, seventh month, third day'. See *The Trial of a Time Lord* 5 (1986).

Tides on Thoros-Beta

The planet Thoros-Beta has distinctive pink seas and a blue-green sky. That sky is dominated by the vast ringed planet Thoros-Alpha, its twin. As we've seen, the close proximity of one world to other massive objects (such as other planets or moons) creates powerful tidal forces that can dramatically affect the landscape. This would have consequences for the native life on the planet, such as the large, slug-like Mentors including Sil. But the Mentors apply technology here.

Arriving on Thoros-Beta at the start of *The Trial of a Time Lord* 5, Peri remarks to the Sixth Doctor that the tides go out very quickly. The Doctor assumes there must be some kind of 'mechanical tide control'. Of course, he's seen something similar on Earth's Moon in the 21st century (see *Tides on the Moon* on page 20). But he seems to be right, and soon discovers sophisticated technology used to extract energy from this sea. The implication is that the technology was built for this extractive purpose, and control of the tides is a side effect rather than the intention.

Speaking of Earth's Moon, the names given to bodies of water on Thoros-Beta are not a million miles away from the names astronomers gave the dark parts of the lunar surface when they were believed to be oceans. Earth's Moon boasts the calm-sounding Sea of Tranquility and Sea of Serenity, and the less-calm Sea of Crisis. On Thoros-Beta, it's *all* crisis in what really are seas. We hear of the Sea of Despair and Longing, the Sea of Turmoil and the Sea of Sorrows.

The irony, of course, is that the technology on Thoros-Beta creates faster tides with smaller, lower waves. Peri's life is threatened when she's chained up to the rocks as a tide comes in. But on the whole, despite the names, these are calmer waters than we have on Earth.

04 JUL none

04 JUL 2025 For the second time this year, this is one of the best evenings in 2025 to view Mercury, the planet closest to our Sun, as it reaches its highest point over the horizon (its 'greatest eastern elongation'). It will appear as a relatively bright star low in the western sky soon after sunset.

05 JUL 2008 *Journey's End*

Donna Noble leaves the TARDIS

06 JUL 1979 A page-a-day calendar in *The Android Invasion* (1975) gives the date as *'July 6 Friday'* – but what year? There were Friday 6 Julys in 1973, 1979 and 1984, and 1979 is the closest of those to Sarah's claim in the previous story: *'I'm from 1980.'* Does that mean this is the year in which the android invasion takes place? Who knows? The calendar might not be very reliable, not least because each page gives the exact same date!

06 JUL 2009 *Torchwood: Children of Earth – Day One*

07 JUL 1919 John Devon Roland 'Jon' Pertwee, who played the Third Doctor

07 JUL 2009 *Torchwood: Children of Earth – Day Two*

08 JUL 2006 *Doomsday*

Rose Tyler leaves the TARDIS

First appearance of temp Donna Noble, who travels with the Tenth and Fourteenth Doctors

08 JUL 2009 *Torchwood: Children of Earth – Day Three*

08 JUL 2022 *Torchwood: Miracle Day – The New World* in US

09 JUL 1966 *The War Machines* 3

09 JUL 2009 *Torchwood: Children of Earth - Day Four*

09 JUL 2011 *Torchwood: Miracle Day - The New World* in Australia and Canada

10 JUL 1965 *The Time Meddler: The Meddling Monk*

10 JUL 2009 *Torchwood: Children of Earth - Day Five*

10 JUL 2025 Full Moon

11 JUL 1964 *The Sensorites: Hidden Danger*

11 JUL 1979 Skylab, the first US space station, re-enters the Earth's atmosphere and burns up - long after its crew have left. The Doctor helped with re-entry, which 'nearly took off my thumb'. See *Tooth and Claw* (2006).

12 JUL none

12 JUL 2025 Delta Aquarids

This meteor shower is produced by the trails of two comets, called Marsden and Kracht. Although the shower lasts for more than a month, even at its peak there are only about 20 meteors per hour - pretty average as meteor showers go. That said, the peak this year, on the night of 28-29 July, coincides with a relatively thin crescent Moon, so there won't be much moonlight to obscure the view. In dark, clear skies this shower could be impressive.

13 JUL 1643 In the midst of the English Civil Wars, a force of parliamentary soldiers and a regiment loyal to King Charles fought at Little Hodcombe – destroying each other and the village. The psychic alien Malus probably didn't help. See *The Awakening* (1984).

13 JUL none

13 JUL 2025 Delta Aquarids

14 JUL 2011 *Torchwood: Miracle Day – The New World* in UK

14 JUL 2025 Delta Aquarids

15 JUL 2011 *Torchwood: Miracle Day – Rendition* in US

15 JUL 2025 Delta Aquarids

We've generally chosen constellations for this book that are visible from the northern hemisphere and specifically from the UK. This month, we're going further afield to look at three groups of stars visible from southern latitudes. The ancient Greeks could see some of these stars, more if they journeyed south, so these stars became associated with voyages into unknown realms and the adventures to be had there.

If we have a view of the southern skies, we can use bright star Sirius in the constellation Canis Major (see page 41) to find these three linked constellations, which the ancient Greeks and Romans thought looked like an enormous ship, the *Argo Navis*. This was the ship of famous hero Jason and his crew, the Argonauts.

But Argo Navis was such a big constellation, containing more than 160 stars visible to the naked eye in dark skies, that later astronomers found it unwieldy. In his 1763 star catalogue, the French astronomer Nicolas-Louis de Lacaille broke the ship up into three sections: the keel (or carina), the stern or poop deck (puppis) and the sails (vela). The Doctor mentions Lacaille and his poop deck in *Rogue* (2024). That pattern of stars can't be seen from the posh house where the ball is being held, so it's the Doctor showing off his extensive knowledge – and perhaps testing the knowledge of who he is speaking to.

Lacaille named 14 of the constellations in the 88 that are officially recognised today. Many of these are in the southern skies and not visible from the northern hemisphere. Whereas older constellations took their names from heroes, creatures and other elements of ancient myth, he preferred to name constellations after scientific instruments.

The Doctor also mentions one of these. The constellation Norma isn't named after a woman. The name refers to a right-angled tool, like a set square or carpenter's square.

16 JUL 1966 *The War Machines* 4

The same day as broadcast, Computer Day, or 'C Day', sees all the world's computers come under the control of an evil AI called WOTAN.

16 JUL 2011 *Torchwood: Miracle Day – Rendition* in Australia and Canada

16 JUL 2025 Delta Aquarids

17 JUL 1965 *The Time Meddler: A Battle of Wits*

17 JUL 2025 Delta Aquarids; Perseids
Produced by the trail of debris from comet Swift-Tuttle, the Perseid meteor shower is usually one of the best to observe. At its peak on the night of 12–13 August, up to 60 meteors can be seen per hour. However, this year that peak coincides with the waning gibbous Moon, which may obscure all but the brightest of meteors. As always, they're best seen in clear, dark skies.

18 JUL 0064 Great Fire of Rome, encouraged by Emperor Nero and inspired by the First Doctor – oops! See *The Romans* (1965).

18 JUL 1964 *The Sensorites: A Race Against Death*

18 JUL 2025 Third Quarter

Delta Aquarids; Perseids

19 JUL none

19 JUL 2025 Delta Aquarids; Perseids

20 JUL 1966 Ben Jackson and Polly join the TARDIS for the first time; on exactly the same date they return to London, battle the Chameleons at Gatwick Airport and go home, while the TARDIS is stolen on the orders of the Daleks – see *The War Machines* (1966), and *The Faceless Ones* and *The Evil of the Daleks* (both 1967).

20 JUL 1969 The first humans land and walk on the Moon, watched live on television by half a billion people on Earth, and by many billions of viewers for years afterwards. That's why the Doctor hides a clip inside this footage, in *Day of the Moon* (2011), ensuring that the maximum number of humans possible will see an instruction to fight the alien Silents.

20 JUL none

20 JUL 2025 Delta Aquarids; Perseids

21 JUL 2011 *Torchwood: Miracle Day – Rendition* in UK

21 JUL 2025 Delta Aquarids; Perseids

22 JUL 1964 Bonita Melody Lysette 'Bonnie' Langford, who plays the Doctor's friend Melanie Bush

22 JUL 1966 UK premiere in London of *Daleks' Invasion Earth 2150 A.D.*, the second movie version of *Doctor Who*, starring Peter Cushing as a human Doctor, this time adapted from TV serial *The Dalek Invasion of Earth* (1964). The leading role of policeman Tom Campbell was played by Bernard Cribbins, 41 years before he played Wilfred Mott, who travelled with the Tenth Doctor.

22 JUL 2011 *Torchwood: Miracle Day – Dead of Night* in US

22 JUL 2025 Delta Aquarids; Perseids

2 JUL 2011 *Torchwood: Miracle Day - Dead of Night* in Australia and Canada

23 JUL 2025 Delta Aquarids; Perseids

24 JUL 1794 The Doctor and his friends arrive in countryside some 12 kilometres from Paris, when France is ruled by zealous revolutionaries. See *The Reign of Terror* (1964).

24 JUL 1965 *The Time Meddler: Checkmate*

24 JUL 2025 New Moon

Delta Aquarids; Perseids

25 JUL 1794 The Doctor's granddaughter Susan and friends Barbara and Ian are incarcerated in Conciergerie Prison in Paris, facing sentences of death; the Doctor meets French statesman Maximilien François Marie Isidore de Robespierre, the so-called tyrant of France. See *The Reign of Terror* (1964)

25 JUL 1964 *Season 1: The Sensorites: Kidnap*

25 JUL 2025 Delta Aquarids; Perseids

26 JUL 1794 Having escaped jail, Susan and Barbara are recaptured, while Ian walks into a trap - though the Doctor reassures his friends that he can still get them all to safety. 'Don't argue,' he tells Barbara. 'You know my plans always work perfectly.' See *The Reign of Terror* (1964).

26 JUL none

26 JUL 2025 Delta Aquarids; Perseids

27 JUL 1794 Arrest of Robespierre, his downfall coinciding with, or part of, the end of the so-called Reign of Terror. Also on this day according to *Doctor Who* – but less evident in historical sources – Paul Barras and Napoleon Bonaparte meet in a pub called *The Sinking Ship* to plan the future of France, as observed by the Doctor's friends Barbara and Ian. See *The Reign of Terror* (1964).

27 JUL 2012 Opening ceremony for London 2012 Summer Olympics begins with the Olympic flame being lit by the Tenth Doctor (according to *Fear Her* (2006)) and closes with Paul McCartney performing the Beatles song 'Hey Jude'.

27 JUL none

27 JUL 2025 Delta Aquarids; Perseids

28 JUL 2011 *Torchwood: Miracle Day – Dead of Night* in UK

28 JUL 2025 Perseids; Delta Aquarids – peaks in the evening (and next morning).

29 JUL 2011 *Torchwood: Miracle Day – Escape to LA* in Australia, Canada and US

29 JUL 2025 Perseids; Delta Aquarids – peaks in the early morning (and previous night).

30 JUL none

30 JUL 2025 Delta Aquarids; Perseids

31 JUL none

31 JUL 2025 Delta Aquarids; Perseids

Why are the months of July and August called that, and how is this related to days being erased from existence – more than once – and other days being repeated? These sound like things from *Doctor Who*, yet they're real and echo in the calendar we still use to mark our journey round and round the Sun. So, here's the whole gorgeous tapestry...

According to ancient legend, Romulus – the founder and first king of Rome – established the Roman calendar that helped his people mark the course of each year, which meant they knew when to sow and harvest the fields. Each year started at the spring equinox (on or close to 21 March in our modern calendar) with 'Mensis Martius' or the month of Mars. Mars was the Roman god of war but also a guardian of farmers, and this ancient name is where we get our word for the same month: March.

There then followed months of Apru aka Aphrodite (goddess of love), from which we get 'April', of Maia (oldest of the Pleiades, see page 232), from which we get 'May', and of Juno (queen of the gods), from which we get 'June'. There were then Mensis Quintilis ('fifth month'), Sextilis ('sixth'), September ('seventh'), October ('eighth'), November ('ninth') and December ('tenth'). Six of these months lasted 30 days, the other four lasted 31, giving a total of 10 months and 304 days in a year.

This is obviously short of the 365 days we know it takes Earth to complete an orbit of the Sun (not including leap years, which we'll come to in a bit). That would mean the Romulan calendar didn't work. For example, one year would begin on or close to modern 21 March but 304 days later the next year would begin on or close to modern 19 January. You'd get very different results from sowing seeds on each of those two dates.

From what we understand from surviving ancient sources, the Romans made the system work anyway. One explanation is that the 304-day calendar left out 60 days of winter, when people didn't do any farming, but there are also examples of the Romans complaining about and revising the system. In 46 BCE, Julius Caesar, who had become dictator of Rome following years of military victories and was known as a great organiser, led a major reform of the calendar. The new system took his name.

The Julian calendar introduced a year lasting an average of 365.25 days, based on how long it took the same patterns of stars to appear in the same part of the sky. To make this Julian calendar practical, three years each lasting exactly 365 days were followed by a 'leap year' of 366.

The new system also introduced two new months before Mensis Martius. The year now began with the first day of Ianuarius, named after Janus (god of beginnings), from which we get 'January'; then there was Februarius, named after a festival held in Rome at that time of year, from which we get 'February'. Martius was now the third of 12 months; Quintilis, meaning 'fifth', was now the seventh month; Sextilis, meaning 'sixth', was now the eighth. This continued with September, October, November and December, yet we still use these names today, an echo of a model of time that was outmoded even in ancient times.

The Romans renamed Quintilis after Julius Caesar (who'd been born in that seventh month) and Sextilis after his successor, Augustus Caesar, from which we get 'July' and 'August'. Augustus was the first Emperor of Rome and the Julian calendar was used across the expanding empire. It's still in use in many cultures, more than 2,000 years later.

But over time it became clear that it doesn't quite match the movement of the fixed pattern of stars. We now know that it takes Earth fractionally less than 365.25 days to complete an orbit of the Sun – the exact amount varies a bit and is currently 365.24 days.

This tiny difference gradually adds up: the Julian calendar gains an extra day every 129 years. Dates for observed phenomena slowly drifted. The spring equinox would occur earlier and earlier in the year, eventually occurring well before 21 March, which caused problems in the calculation of the date of Easter (see page 73). Revisions to the system were constantly needed.

Then, in 1582, the Catholic Church in Rome issued a new rule to correct the system by slightly reducing the number of leap years. In the Julian system, a leap year takes place *every* four years. In the later system, a leap year is:

- Any year exactly divisible by four (such as 2024 – a leap year)
- *Unless* it is also exactly divisible by 100 (such as 2100 – *not* a leap year)
- *Unless* it is also exactly divisible by 400 (such as 2000 – a leap year)

In issuing these complicated new rules, Pope Gregory XIII also decreed that, to make the spring equinox match up with 21 March again, 10 days would be erased from time. In the Catholic world, Thursday 4 October 1582 was followed immediately by Friday 15 October. The new system, now known as the Gregorian calendar after the pope who issued the rules, also slightly changed the way Easter was calculated.

Over time, non-Catholic countries saw the sense in converting to the more accurate Gregorian system. In 1752, Britain and its empire (which at that point included what are now the United States) made the switch. To synchronise with other countries already using the Gregorian calendar, Britain (and its empire) had to erase *11* days from time: Wednesday 2 September was followed the next day by Thursday 14 September. Bad news for anyone with a birthday between those two dates!

The switch was brought about by a new law, which also added a few other rules. First, it established the date on which the year started in Britain (and its empire). For centuries, the 'legal' year began on 25 March, so that 24 March 1750 was followed by 25 March 1751. In 1600, Scotland followed many other countries in switching to 1 January as the start of the year, based on the old Roman system. England and Wales continued using 25 March, and it's common to see documents from the time using a double system: 24 March $17\frac{50}{51}$, as if the same day occurred simultaneously in two different years.

Changing the day on which a new year started required further synchronisation, so 1751 ran from 25 March to 31 December, and lasted just 282 days. (1752 ran for 354 days with the 11 erased from September, and then things settled down.)

Lastly, the new law set the date for the extra day in leap years as 29 February. Before this, the practice had been to follow 24 February in a leap year with *another* 24 February, effectively meaning that everyone got to live the same day twice.

♥♥+
AUGUST

🚪 First reference to the Doctor's home planet, later named as Gallifrey. Susan says: 'It's quite like Earth but at night the sky is a burned orange and the leaves on the trees are bright silver.'

Descriptions of Gallifrey

We've seen the Doctor's adopted home planet in numerous stories but often it's at its most vivid when he hear the Doctor describe it.

'When I was a little boy, we used to live in a house that was perched halfway up the top of a mountain,' says the Third Doctor in *The Time Monster* (1972). Behind the house, among the bare rocks and patches of snow, an old hermit lived under a tree and taught the Doctor to see the beauty and colour of the world around them. We see something like this landscape in the Death Zone, featured in *The Five Doctors* (1983).

Seen from space, though, Gallifrey is an orange or scarlet world – see *The Invasion of Time* (1978) and *The End of Time* (2009-2010). The domain immediately outside the huge Citadel complex is a desert of yellowish sand, known as the Dry Lands and first seen in *The Invasion of Time*. In *The Sound of Drums* (2007), the Tenth Doctor says that this Citadel is located among the Mountains of Solace and Solitude on the Continent of Wild Endeavour.

The Master's father owned lands on the slopes of Mount Perdition including pastures of red grass, described in *The End of Time* (2009-2010).

The Eighth Doctor recalls a 'warm Gallifreyan night' lying back in the grass with his father watching a vivid, rich meteor storm, the sky dancing with lights of myriad colours. 'The second sun would rise in the south and the mountains would shine,' the Tenth Doctor tells Martha Jones in *Gridlock* (2007). 'The leaves on the trees were silver, and when they caught the light every morning, it looked like a forest on fire. When the autumn came, the breeze would blow through the branches like a song.'

01 AUG 2025 First Quarter

Delta Aquarids; Perseids

02 AUG none

02 AUG 2025 Delta Aquarids; Perseids

03 AUG none

03 AUG 2025 Delta Aquarids; Perseids

04 AUG 1987 Ruth Madeley, who plays Shirley Anne Bingham, 56th scientific adviser to UNIT

04 AUG 2011 *Torchwood: Miracle Day – Escape to LA* in UK

04 AUG 2025 Delta Aquarids; Perseids

05 AUG 2011 *Torchwood: Miracle Day – The Categories of Life* in US

05 AUG 2025 Delta Aquarids; Perseids

06 AUG 1496 The TARDIS materialises inside the tomb of High Priestess Yetaxa in an Aztec city in what's now Mexico. When the Doctor's friend Barbara dons a bracelet from the tomb and steps out into the city, she is mistaken for Yetaxa, now reborn as a god. See *The Aztecs* (1964).

06 AUG 2011 *Torchwood: Miracle Day – The Categories of Life* in Australia and Canada

06 AUG 2025 Delta Aquarids; Perseids

07 AUG 1496 The First Doctor makes cocoa for himself and an Aztec woman called Cameca and discovers that, according to local custom, they've just become engaged. See *The Aztecs* (1964).

07 AUG none

07 AUG 2025 Delta Aquarids; Perseids

08 AUG 1496 A real-life solar eclipse in what's now Mexico means we can date the events of *The Aztecs: The Day of Darkness* (1964). We can even estimate what time of day the events happened, as the real-life eclipse began at 14:36 – local time in what's now Mexico City – and lasted some five and a half minutes. Just enough time for the First Doctor and his companions to escape back to the TARDIS.

Like a lunar eclipse (see page 53), a solar eclipse occurs when the orbits of the Earth, Sun and Moon mean that all three bodies briefly line up. In a solar eclipse, the Moon is directly between the Earth and the Sun, blocking the glare of sunlight. The Moon is 40 times smaller than the Sun but also 40 times closer to Earth, so almost perfectly covers the disc of the Sun, allowing us to see (and study) the Sun's outer atmosphere, the corona.

The Moon's orbit around the Earth is not a perfect circle so sometimes the Moon is slightly closer to us during a solar eclipse. When this happens, a ring of bright sunlight can be seen around the Moon. This is called an 'annular' eclipse, after the Latin word for 'ring'.

We see a regular rather than annular eclipse in *The Day of Darkness*. Which is a shame, given that the Doctor got engaged the previous day.

08 AUG 1964 *The Reign of Terror: A Land of Fear*

08 AUG 2025 Delta Aquarids; Perseids

09 AUG none

09 AUG 2025 Full Moon

09 AUG 2025 Delta Aquarids; Perseids

10 AUG 1968 *The Dominators* 1

Delta Aquarids; Perseids

11 AUG 2011 *Torchwood: Miracle Day – The Categories of Life* in UK

11 AUG 2025 Delta Aquarids; Perseids

12 AUG 2011 *Torchwood: Miracle Day – The Middle Men* in US

12 AUG 2025 Delta Aquarids; Perseids – peaks this evening (and tomorrow morning).

13 AUG 2011 *Torchwood: Miracle Day – The Middle Men* in Australia and Canada

13 AUG 2025 Delta Aquarids; Perseids – peaks this morning (and last night).

14 AUG none

14 AUG 2025 Delta Aquarids; Perseids

15 AUG 1964 *The Reign of Terror: Guests of Madame Guillotine*

15 AUG 2025 Delta Aquarids; Perseids

A Holiday for the Doctor

You'll probably have noticed that August is a bit sparse for episodes of *Doctor Who*. Over more than 60 years, series tend to run in spring, autumn and / or winter but – on the whole – the Doctor takes the summer off.

In 1968, the production team came up with a clever way to bridge the nine-week gap over the summer between Seasons 5 and 6 of *Doctor Who*. They would – get this! – fill the gap by *repeating* a *Doctor Who* story.

At the time, this was quite a big deal. Until that point, just one episode of *Doctor Who* had been repeated on British TV – the very first episode, shown again a week later because it was felt that it had been overshadowed by news of the assassination of US President John F Kennedy. Repeats of *any* programme were relatively rare and there were strict rules about how many programmes the BBC could repeat in a year.

Even so, the powers-that-be agreed to a repeat of seven-episode story *The Evil of the Daleks* and the production team found an ingenious way to explain what was happening to the audience.

At the end of *The Wheel In Space* 6 (1 June 1968), space librarian Zoe Heriot stows away on board the TARDIS, keen to join the Doctor on his adventures. He feels he should warn her about the potential dangers, and so dons a headset that allows him to share his thought patterns on a screen. 'I'm going to weave them into a complete story for you,' he says. 'Have you ever heard of the Daleks?' The screen then shows a brief sequence from the first episode of *The Evil of the Daleks*.

The following week, on 8 June, the BBC repeated that whole episode, with new dialogue added over the opening theme between the Doctor and Zoe to remind viewers that the Doctor was sharing these memories.

The repeats continued on 15 and 22 June, followed by a two-week break to allow for the BBC's live coverage of the tennis tournament held in Wimbledon. The remaining four episodes of *The Evil of the Daleks* were then repeated from 13 July to 3 August 1968. The following week, the new series of *Doctor Who* began with the opening episode of *The Dominators*, in which the Doctor is a little weary. 'It's a very exhausting business projecting all those mental images, you know,' he says.

Over the next few years, the summer gap in *Doctor Who* would often be covered by repeats – either whole serials or edited versions. But this idea of the Doctor explaining why stories were being repeated wasn't used again. That is, until 2023 when each episode of *Tales of the TARDIS* on BBC iPlayer featured a similar kind of framing device.

✳✲
✩ **This month's constellation: Cassiopeia**

CASSIOPEIA

CAPH

Another easy-to-spot constellation, with five bright stars making up a distinctive W shape in the northern sky. It's pretty much on the opposite side of Polaris (the North Star) from the Plough in Ursa Major (see page 67). As seen from most of the northern hemisphere, it never sets.

Both Ursa Major and Cassiopeia are ancient constellations, the earliest known record of them in the star catalogue *Almagest* compiled by Greek-Egyptian astronomer Claudius Ptolemy in about 150 CE, but based on earlier traditions. Ptolemy listed 48 constellations; all but one of these is included in the 88 internationally recognised constellations today. (As we saw last month, the huge boat Argo Navis was broken up into three smaller patterns.)

Ptolemy identified this W-shaped constellation as a seated figure: Cassiopeia, Queen of Ethiopia, on her throne. Today, there's a country in Africa called Ethiopia but we're not sure that this is where Cassiopeia came from. The word 'Ethiopia' had a broader meaning to the ancient Greeks, literally meaning 'burnt face'; in this context, they used 'Ethiopia' in the sense of 'place where people have darker skin than is common in ancient Greece', meaning Africa in general. Some historical sources seem to use 'Ethiopia' to include parts of the Mediterranean coast such as modern Jordan and Israel.

Wherever she came from, the suggestion is that these distinctive stars represent an important black woman from ancient history.

Cassiopeia is one of a number of characters from a particular Greek myth or story who have constellations named after them. There's also Cassiopeia's husband King Cepheus, their daughter Andromeda, her boyfriend, the hero Perseus, and the sea monster he battled, Cetus.

In *Logopolis* (1981), the Fourth Doctor and his archenemy the Master work together to transmit a computer program from the radio telescope at Jodrell Bank in Cheshire to a 'charged vacuum emboitement' (a void opened into another universe) located in Cassiopeia, in a desperate bid to prevent the collapse of all of time and space.

📅 16 AUG 2017

'Holiday liner sinks, many feared lost' reads the headline of a tragic story reported by journalist Peter Peyton and published in an unnamed newspaper under the date 'Friday, August 16 2017' – though 16 August 2017 was actually a Wednesday.

In 2018, a fragment of this story, including the date, is discovered by a man called Swann, who has been living deep underground for five years in the belief that a global nuclear war has left the Earth's surface uninhabitable, with 'radiation everywhere'. 'How can there be holiday liners?' asks the incredulous Swann, realising he has been lied to. See *The Enemy of the World* (1967–68).

16 AUG none

16 AUG 2025 Third Quarter

Delta Aquarids; Perseids

17 AUG 1947 The Thirteenth Doctor and her friends arrive near the new border between India and Pakistan, days after the partitioning of the two countries, hoping to look into Yasmin Khan's family history. But they soon find the body of a murdered man, and encounter two alien assassins – the Thijarians. See *Demons of the Punjab* (2018).

17 AUG 1968 *The Dominators* 2

17 AUG 2025 Delta Aquarids; Perseids

18 AUG 1572 King Henry III of Navarre, a leading figure among a group of French Protestants called Huguenots, marries the Catholic Princess Margaret of Valois at a ceremony held in Paris. Many eminent Huguenots come to Paris for the wedding. This does not please Margaret's Catholic family, including her brother Charles IX, King of France, and her mother Catherine de' Medici, Queen of France. Tensions are left simmering over the next few hot summer days. See *The Massacre* (1966).

18 AUG 1947 The Thirteenth Doctor officiates the wedding of Yasmin Khan's grandmother Umbreen, a Muslim, to a young Hindu man called Prem. But Prem's brother Manish opposes the wedding – and he is not alone. See *Demons of the Punjab* (2018).

18 AUG 1951 Barbara and Eddie Smith, the parents of three-month-old baby Sarah Jane, are tragically killed when their car collides with a tractor, as seen in *The Sarah Jane Adventures: The Temptation of Sarah Jane Smith* (2008). Sarah is brought up by her aunt, the virologist Lavinia Smith, later posing as her to gain access to a UNIT facility, where she first meets the Doctor. See *The Time Warrior* (1973).

18 AUG 2011 *Torchwood: Miracle Day – The Middle Men* in UK

18 AUG 2025 Delta Aquarids; Perseids

19 AUG 2011 *Torchwood: Miracle Day – Immortal Sins* in US

19 AUG 2025 Again, this could be one of the best mornings of 2025 to view planet Mercury as it reaches 'greatest western elongation', or its highest point above the horizon in the dawn sky. Look out for a relatively bright star low in the eastern sky just before sunrise.

Delta Aquarids; Perseids

🎂 **20 AUG 1943** Anthony Ainley, who played the Doctor's enemy the Master in stories broadcast in the 1980s

Percy James Patrick Kent-Smith aka Sylvester McCoy, who plays the Seventh Doctor

20 AUG 1962 Sophie Aldred, who plays the Doctor's friend Ace

Survival (1989) features actors playing the Doctor, companion and main villain who all share a birthday!

📺🔝 **20 AUG 2011** *Torchwood: Miracle Day – Immortal Sins* in Australia and Canada

☄️ **20 AUG 2025** Delta Aquarids; Perseids

📅 **21 AUG 1572** The First Doctor and Steven Taylor arrive in Paris and are soon caught up in the simmering tensions between Catholics and Protestants. See *The Massacre* (1966).

📺 **21 AUG** none

☄️ **21 AUG 2025** Delta Aquarids; Perseids

📅 **22 AUG 1572** In Paris, the Doctor's friend Steven Taylor learns of a Catholic plot to assassinate a leading Protestant figure who the conspirators refer to only as the 'Sea Beggar'. See *The Massacre* (1966).

📺 **22 AUG 1964** *The Reign of Terror: A Change of Identity*

22 AUG 2025 Delta Aquarids; Perseids

23 AUG 0079 The Tenth Doctor and Donna Noble arrive in the Roman city of Pompeii, the day before the volcanic eruption of nearby Mount Vesuvius buries the city – a fixed point in history the Doctor cannot change. See *The Fires of Pompeii* (2008).

23 AUG 1572 Charles IX, the Catholic King of France, orders the deaths of leading Huguenots, which sparks widespread mob violence. 'The massacre continued for several days in Paris and then spread to other parts of France,' the First Doctor tells Steven Taylor as they escape. He thinks some 10,000 people died in Paris alone, and concludes that 'history sometimes gives us a terrible shock', but he dare not change the course of established events. See *The Massacre* (1966).

23 AUG 1965 Premiere in London of *Dr Who and the Daleks*, a film adaptation of the TV serial *The Daleks* (1963–1964), starring Peter Cushing as a human version of the Doctor, accompanied by granddaughters Susan and Barbara, and Barbara's boyfriend Ian.

23 AUG 2014 *Deep Breath*

First appearance of Missy

23 AUG 2025 New Moon

Delta Aquarids; Perseids

24 AUG 0079

The Tenth Doctor and Donna witness the eruption of Mount Vesuvius. The Doctor can't change history and save the whole town, but Donna persuades him to save someone. They go back and rescue the friends they've made – marble trader Lobus Caecilius and his family. See *The Fires of Pompeii* (2008).

Donna's intervention seems to haunt the Doctor for several lifetimes. In *The Girl Who Died* (2015), we learn it informs the face subconsciously chosen by the Twelfth Doctor during his regeneration.

24 AUG 1968 *The Dominators*

By mistake, the opening titles give the name of the overall story but not that this is Episode 3 (of five).

24 AUG 2025 Perseids

25 AUG 1975 Bank holiday programme Disney Time presented by the Fourth Doctor before he receives an urgent summons from the Brigadier at UNIT – leading directly into the next episode of *Doctor Who*, broadcast five days later.

Disney Who

Today, new episodes of *Doctor Who* are broadcast in the UK and Ireland by the BBC and to the rest of the world by Disney+. But *Doctor Who*'s relationship with the Walt Disney Company goes back much further than that.

+   **25 AUG 1975** The Fourth Doctor presents *Disney Time*, introducing cartoons and clips from films.

+ **30 MAR 1985** The Sixth Doctor wears various different cat badges on the lapel of his distinctive, multicoloured coat. In *Revelation of the Daleks* (1985) – and especially visible in Part Two – he wears a badge of Marie, a kitten from Disney's 1970 animated film *The Aristocats*.

+ **23 JAN 1994** The Seventh Doctor appears on ITV programme *The Disney Club*.

+ **25 DEC 2005** The newly regenerated Tenth Doctor realises he is inadvertently quoting words from Disney's 1994 animated film *The Lion King*.

25 AUG 2011 *Torchwood: Miracle Day – Immortal Sins* in UK

26 AUG 1989 Tides on Spiridon

The planet Spiridon is a world of dense jungle full of dangerous plants and creatures. There's also the odd phenomenon of pools of molten ice. These sustain sub-zero temperatures but remain semi-liquid.

In *Planet of the Daleks*, a group of Thals from the planet Skaro have studied the geology of Spiridon. They think there's much more of this molten ice under the planet's surface and that it periodically erupts in tremendous explosions. The effect is something like a volcano, but with molten ice instead of white-hot lava. The Thals and the Doctor hope to cause an eruption that will thwart a Dalek plot.

Now, we don't learn enough about Spiridon in this story to know what sparks these natural eruptions of molten ice. It may be that Spiridon has one or more moons, or that its orbit takes it close to other massive neighbours that generate the kind of tidal heating we see on Androzani Minor (see page 86). It might be that eruptions on Spiridon have nothing to do with tidal forces. But the remarkable thing is that this extraordinary phenomenon invented in a 1973 *Doctor Who* story turns out to be something that's happening in our Solar System.

On 26 August 1989, the *Voyager 2* space probe saw evidence of an eruption on Triton, moon of Neptune. Suspecting that this was an *icy* eruption, scientists coined the term 'cryovolcanism', meaning 'ice volcano'. It's caused by tidal flexing – as Triton orbits Neptune, the planet's mavity stretches the moon one way and then another. This creates heat deep within Triton, which keeps its underground oceans liquid under the ice. The effect is increased by its translucent crust of frozen nitrogen providing a warming 'greenhouse' effect.

What's more, in November 2005, the *Cassini* space probe photographed geysers of water ice erupting from the surface of Enceladus, moon of Saturn, thought to be the result of tidal flexing caused by its close relationship to another large moon, Dione. We think something similar is happening on Europa, one of the moons of Jupiter, but so far have only circumstantial evidence.

On dwarf plants Ceres and Pluto, and perhaps on Titan (a moon of Saturn) and Charon (moon of Pluto), chemicals with a lower freezing point than water ooze onto the surface in a manner rather like what we see happening on Spiridon. There's evidence that cryovolcanism also took place in the ancient past on Ganymede (another moon of Jupiter) and Miranda (a moon of Uranus).

But here's a thing. New scientific terms such as 'cryovolcanism' are usually assigned by the first person to observe the particular phenomenon. 'Cryovolcanism' was used to describe what was seen on Triton in 1989. But *Doctor Who* writers were on to this long before that, and came up with a name we should perhaps be using instead.

On page 13 of *The Dalek Outer Space Book*, published in 1966, the term used is 'Icano'; modified as 'icecano' when featured on page 21 of *Terry Nation's Dalek Annual 1977* (published in 1976).

26 AUG 2011 *Torchwood: Miracle Day - End of the Road* in US

27 AUG 1883 Rose Tyler learns from Clive on or just before 6 March 2005 that the Ninth Doctor washed up on the island of Sumatra in 1883, 'on the very day Krakatoa exploded'. See *Rose* (2005).

In fact, the island of Krakatoa in the Sundai Strait between Sumatra and Java suffered a series of eruptions between May and October of that year, but the worst were the four explosions on 27 August - the third of which, at 10.02 am, was heard almost 5,000 km away. More than 36,000 people are thought to have been killed, perhaps many times more.

27 AUG 1962 Wilfred Mott's friend Minnie Hooper is briefly locked inside a (real) police box due to 'misbehaving', as she gleefully recalls in *The End of Time* 1 (2009).

Real police boxes

We learn in the second ever episode of *Doctor Who* that the TARDIS should be able to change its exterior appearance, disguising itself when and wherever it goes. 'It's been an ionic column and a sedan chair' before settling in the guise of a police box, says the Doctor's granddaughter Susan.

When *Doctor Who* began, the police box was a perfectly ordinary bit of street furniture in many towns and cities across the UK, as familiar to viewers as a post box. In the days before walkie-talkies, let alone mobile phones, they were a means for the public to call on help with a direct line to the local police station, and a base for police constables patrolling a beat. Inside a real police box, you'd find a desk, stool, fire extinguisher and first-aid kit, and perhaps an electric heater to warm the poor constable on cold nights. (Several PCs complained that police boxes were cold and damp.) It was a fun idea to suggest that such a familiar and ordinary object on city streets was, in fact, a spaceship – originally, just for one story.

'What happened was that we had a very small budget and we couldn't afford to keep building new exteriors to the TARDIS,' remembered Doctor Who's first producer Verity Lambert in an interview published in 1983. 'But that turned out, I think, to be a positive advantage because there was a kind of incongruity of this police telephone box appearing in the French Revolution and the middle of Neanderthal man.' The wrongness of seeing such a familiar object in unlikely locations became part of the appeal.

The first (real) police boxes were red, cast-iron constructions installed in Glasgow in 1891. A number of different designs were tried, and the TARDIS is based on the 1929 model by architect Gilbert Mackenzie Trench. Earlier versions were often made of wood, but the new model was a concrete box, 2.8 metres tall and 1.4 metres wide, with the telephone behind a panel on the left-hand side of the front. The right-hand side of the front was a wooden door that opened outwards.

It says something about the Doctor that in more than 60 years of TV adventures, the TARDIS has never quite matched a real-life police box. Indeed, 'Your spaceship's made of wood,' observes Martha Jones in Smith and Jones (2007).

27 AUG 2011 *Let's Kill Hitler* in UK and
Torchwood: Miracle Day – End of the Road in Australia and
Canada

28 AUG none

29 AUG 1964 *The Reign of Terror: The Tyrant of France*

30 AUG 1975 *Terror of the Zygons* 1

30 AUG 1980 *The Leisure Hive* 1

30 AUG 2003 Yasmin Finney, who plays Rose Noble, daughter of Donna Noble and friend of the Fourteenth and Fifteenth Doctors

30 AUG 2014 *Into the Dalek*

31 AUG 1968 *The Dominators* 4

31 AUG 2025 First Quarter

♥♥+
SEPTEMBER

01 SEP 1979 *Destiny of the Daleks* 1

First appearance of a new incarnation of Romana

01 SEP 2011 *Torchwood: Miracle Day – End of the Road* in UK

01 SEP 2012 *Asylum of the Daleks*

First appearance of junior entertainment manager Oswin Oswald, the first we see of many splinters in time and space of the Doctor's friend Clara Oswald.

02 SEP 1666 While the Fifth Doctor battles three Terileptils, a dropped torch starts a fire. Exacerbated by an exploding energy weapon, the blaze begins the Great Fire of London. See *The Visitation* (1982).

02 SEP 1967 *The Tomb of the Cybermen* 1

02 SEP 1978 *The Ribos Operation* 1

First appearance of Time Lady Romanadvoratrelundar, or 'Romana', who travels with the Fourth Doctor

02 SEP 2011 *Torchwood: Miracle Day – The Gathering* in US

03 SEP 1977 *Horror of Fang Rock* 1

03 SEP 2011 *Night Terrors* in UK and *Torchwood: Miracle Day - The Gathering* in Australia and Canada

04 SEP 1976 *The Masque of Mandragora* 1

05 SEP 1964 *The Reign of Terror: A Bargain of Necessity*

06 SEP 1975 *Terror of the Zygons* 2

06 SEP 1980 *The Leisure Hive* 2

06 SEP 1986 *The Trial of a Time Lord* 1

First appearance of the Valeyard

06 SEP 1989 *Battlefield* 1

06 SEP 2014 *Robot of Sherwood*

07 SEP 1901 Date of the *Daily Telegraph* newspaper containing reports on the assassination of US President William McKinley the previous day and also that the 'First British submarine launched', as found by the Fifth Doctor in a room aboard a yacht, and an important clue about when and where the TARDIS has landed in *Enlightenment* 1 (1983).

In fact, HM *submarine Torpedo Boat No 1* aka *Holland 1*, the first submarine commissioned by the Royal Navy, was launched almost a month later on 2 October. The mix-up may be further evidence that all is not as it appears on this yacht. Or the art department involved in making this episode made up a 'prop' newspaper from separate, real editions.

07 SEP 1968 *The Dominators* 5

07 SEP 1987 *Time and the Rani* 1

First appearance of the Seventh Doctor

07 SEP 2025 Full Moon

Total lunar eclipse seen from Asia, Australia and central and eastern Africa and Europe. As the Moon passes completely through the shadow cast by the Earth, it turns a rusty red colour.

Taurids

This is a minor meteor shower with between five and 10 meteors per hour. Unfortunately, this year, the peak on the night of 4–5 November coincides with the Full Moon, so only the brightest meteors will be visible. But the Taurid meteor shower also lasts for just over two months. One reason for this is that it is produced by the debris from two separate objects: the asteroid 2004 TG10 and comet 2P Encke.

What's the difference? Comets are relatively small, icy bodies that warm up as their orbit takes them closer to the Sun. This produces gases, which extend from the comet in a cloudy trail known as a 'coma'. They can also have a separate 'tail' of debris, blown out by solar radiation and the solar wind.

Asteroids are larger, bulkier objects – effectively, minor planets. We currently know of about a million asteroids in the Solar System, most of them in a belt between the orbits of Mars and Jupiter. Asteroid 2004 TG10 is 1.32 km in diameter and classified as both a Near Earth Asteroid (NEA) and Potentially Hazardous Asteroid (PHA) because its orbit will bring it relatively close to Earth four times in the next 200 years:

11 July 2068 – 21,312,366 km from Earth
16 Nov 2111 – 23,244,943 km
07 Nov 2148 – 10,767,750 km
11 Nov 2198 – 15,967,772 km

Don't worry: that's still quite a distance. For comparison, the Moon is an average 384,400 km from Earth. But given the damage these NEAs and PHAs could do to us on Earth, it's worth our keeping tabs on them all the same.

08 SEP 1979 *Destiny of the Daleks* 2

08 SEP 2011 *Torchwood: Miracle Day – The Gathering* in UK

08 SEP 2012 *Dinosaurs on a Spaceship*

08 SEP 2025 Taurids

09 SEP 1953 Janet Claire Mahoney aka Janet Fielding, who plays the Doctor's friend Tegan Jovanka

09 SEP 1967 *The Tomb of the Cybermen* 2

09 SEP 1978 *The Ribos Operation* 2

09 SEP 2011 *Torchwood: Miracle Day – The Blood Line* in US

09 SEP 2025 Taurids

10 SEP 1966 *The Smugglers* 1

10 SEP 1977 *Horror of Fang Rock* 2

10 SEP 2011 *The Girl Who Waited* in UK and *Torchwood: Miracle Day – The Blood Line* in Australia and Canada

10 SEP 2025 Taurids

11 SEP 1960 Ellie Ravenwood, later Oswald, mum of the Doctor's friend Clara – *The Rings of Akhaten* (2013)

11 SEP 1965 *Galaxy 4: Four Hundred Dawns*

11 SEP 1976 *The Masque of Mandragora* 2

11 SEP 2025 Taurids

12 SEP 1964 *The Reign of Terror: Prisoners of Conciergerie*

12 SEP 19?? Soldiers from the 22nd century travel back in time to this day in the late 1970s or early 1980s to assassinate British diplomat Sir Reginald Styles, to prevent the terrible future they know where the Earth is conquered by the Daleks. See *Day of the Daleks* (1972) and also UNIT dating, page 82.

12 SEP 2025 Taurids

13 SEP 1975 *Terror of the Zygons* 3

13 SEP 19?? On this day in either the late 1970s or early 1980s, soldiers from the 22nd century try a second time to assassinate British diplomat Sir Reginald Styles – but find the Third Doctor and Jo Grant waiting for them instead. See *Day of the Daleks* (1972).

13 SEP 1980 *The Leisure Hive* 3

13 SEP 1986 *The Trial of a Time Lord* 2

13 SEP 1989 *Battlefield* 2

13 SEP 2014 *Listen*

13 SEP 2025 Taurids

14 SEP 1968 *The Mind Robber* 1

14 SEP 19?? On this day, UNIT soldiers battle Organs and Daleks in the grounds of Auderly House, where – ironically – a peace conference is meant to be taking place. See *Day of the Daleks* (1972).

14 SEP 1987 *Time and the Rani* 2

14 SEP 2025 Third Quarter

Taurids

15 SEP 1954 Peter Alan Tyler, father of the Doctor's friend Rose – *Father's Day* (2005)

15 SEP 1979 *Destiny of the Daleks* 3

15 SEP 2011 *Torchwood: Miracle Day – The Blood Line* in UK

15 SEP 2012 *A Town Called Mercy*

15 SEP 2025 Taurids

This month's constellation: Draco

This month's constellation is made up of relatively faint stars, so is trickier to see than some others we've encountered so far.

'Draco' is the ancient Greek and Roman name for a serpent or dragon, which is what ancient people saw in this pattern of stars. They weave between the much more distinct Ursa Major and Ursa Minor (see page 68), which will help you find this constellation.

Its brightest point, Thuban ('head of the serpent'), is a blue-white star. Between 3942 and 1793 BCE, Earth's north pole pointed in this direction, making Thuban the pole star. During this period, the pyramids of Egypt were built, and it's thought that each one was built so that Thuban would be visible at night from the entrance passageway.

Since those ancient times, a gradual shift in the Earth's rotational axis has meant Thuban is no longer directly over the north pole. That distinction is now held by Polaris, the so-called North Star, in the constellation of Ursa Minor. But continuing shifts in Earth's rotational axis mean that Thuban will be the North Star again, in about 19,000 years.

Presumably, given the name, the planet Draconia orbits one of the stars in this constellation. The Third Doctor visits Draconia at some point in the 26th century, when its noble people are on the brink of war with Earth – see *Frontier in Space* (1973). In fact, the Doctor reveals that he is himself a noble of Draconia, the honour having been bestowed on him by the planet's Fifteenth Emperor some 500 years previously. That means the Doctor is on Draconia sometime in the 21st century. Perhaps he's there right now.

16 SEP 1967 *The Tomb of the Cybermen* 3

16 SEP 1978 *The Ribos Operation* 3

16 SEP 2025 Taurids

17 SEP 1966 *The Smugglers* 2

17 SEP 1977 *Horror of Fang Rock* 3

17 SEP 2011 *The God Complex*

17 SEP 2025 Taurids

18 SEP 1965 *Galaxy 4: Trap of Steel*

18 SEP 1976 *The Masque of Mandragora* 3

1ˢᵗ First mention that the Doctor's friends (and we) hear languages translated into English, later explained – in *The End of the World* (2005) – as being done by the TARDIS

18 SEP 2025 Taurids

19 SEP 2015 *The Magician's Apprentice*

19 SEP 2025 Taurids

20 SEP 1975 *Terror of the Zygons* 4

Harry Sullivan leaves the TARDIS

20 SEP 1980 *The Leisure Hive* 4

20 SEP 1986 *The Trial of a Time Lord* 3

20 SEP 1989 *Battlefield* 3

20 SEP 2014 *Time Heist*

20 SEP 2025 Taurids

21 SEP 1968 *The Mind Robber* 2

21 SEP 1987 *Time and the Rani* 3

21 SEP 2025 New Moon

21 SEP 2025 Partial solar eclipse seen in New Zealand (where 76 per cent of the Sun will be obscured), the southern Pacific and Antarctica. A solar eclipse is caused when the Moon passes between Earth and the Sun, blocking sunlight.

Tonight is the best evening in the year to view and photograph the planet Saturn at its closest approach to Earth – or, as astronomers say, 'at opposition' – with its face fully lit by the Sun. On a clear, dark night, with a medium-sized telescope, you should be able to see Saturn's rings and its brightest moons.

Taurids

21 SEP 2360 Alderin Beta is boring, says the Eleventh Doctor, dismissing it as 'planet of the chip shops'. Even so, every world has something going for it. On this one, there's a notable mountain in the middle of a sea. From the clifftop on the north side of the mountain grows an enormous tree, 120 metres (400 feet) tall. Take the lift to the top of the tree and look directly up at 00:12 on this particular day, and you can see more stars in one sky than you can at any other moment in the history of the universe.

'It's like daylight, only magic,' enthuses the Eleventh Doctor. 'You could read a book by it.'* Imagine that – reading *this* book, by starlight.

22 SEP 1944 Frazer Simpson Frederick Hines, who plays the Doctor's friend Jamie McCrimmon

---

* In *Night and the Doctor – First Night*, a bonus scene included on the DVD and Blu-ray releases for Series 6 (2011).

22 SEP 1979 *Destiny of the Daleks* 4

22 SEP 1982 Billie Paul Piper, who plays the Doctor's friend Rose Tyler

22 SEP 2012 *The Power of Three*

First appearance of Kate Lethbridge-Stewart, chief scientific officer at UNIT

22 SEP 2025 Autumnal equinox in northern hemisphere and vernal or spring equinox in southern hemisphere. Equinox, from the Latin for 'equal night', means there are almost equal amounts of daylight and night. In the northern hemisphere, from this point on there will be more night than daylight, and in the southern hemisphere there will be more daylight and night, continuing until the solstice on 21 December.

Taurids

23 SEP 1967 *The Tomb of the Cybermen* 4

23 SEP 1978 *The Ribos Operation* 4

23 SEP 2025 The best day of the year to view and photograph planet Neptune at its closest approach to Earth (what astronomers call 'at opposition') and fully illuminated by the Sun. Even so, this giant blue planet is extremely distant – 4.3 billion km or 2.7 billion miles at this closest point – which means that with the most powerful telescopes it still only appears as a small blue dot.

≋ Tides on Alzarius

What we know about Neptune can help us better understand the ecology of planet Alzarius, located in the exo-space/time continuum outside our own universe and seen in *Full Circle* (1980). The people on Alzarius have long planned to get away. For 4,000 generations, they've maintained and repaired every item on their Starliner spaceship so they're ready to go at a moment's notice.

They want to leave Alzarius to avoid a dangerous natural phenomenon. Every 50 Earth years or so, as Decider Login explains to the Fourth Doctor, 'another planet takes Alzarius away from its sun'. This results in the warm, sunny world undergoing a 'cooling process' resulting in 'Mistfall'. The marshes bubble away, producing thick mist – unhelpfully concealing the huge spiders and Marshmen that then emerge to prey on the people.

Is this a tidal process? Login's explanation suggests that Mistfall is caused by Alzarius moving further away from its sun. That implies the process is seasonal – though seasons on Earth are caused by the tilt of Earth's axis of rotation with respect to the Sun, not by how far away we are. We learn later in *Full Circle* that Login doesn't understand the process of Mistfall completely, so perhaps his explanation isn't quite what's happening.

The reference to another planet affecting Alzarius suggests perturbation. This is where one body orbiting another is affected by a third body. We now know that several bodies in the Solar System are close enough to perturb one another on a regular basis, and that this leads to their orbits becoming synchronised in a manner called 'orbital resonance'.

The four largest moons in orbit around Jupiter are a good example. Of these, Io is the closest to Jupiter, completing four orbits of the planet in 7.2 Earth days. In exactly the same period, Europa completes two orbits and Ganymede one. Callisto completes almost 43 per cent of an orbit in the same time.

As we saw in *Tides on Androzani Minor* (p. 86), the proximity of these different moons and their mavitational forces creates tidal flexing in each of them, with dramatic volcanic effects on Io.

Saturn has at least three pairs of moons in orbital resonance: Mimas and Tethys; Enceladus and Dione; Titan and Hyperion. The gaps in Saturn's famous rings are also the result of orbital resonance with Mimas.

It happens with planets, too – which is where Neptune comes in. After the planet Uranus was discovered in 1781, astronomers noted that it sped up and slowed down as it orbited the Sun. The likeliest explanation for this strange behaviour was that it was being perturbed by another, more distant planet we hadn't discovered yet.

The French astronomer Urbain Le Verrier undertook the complex mathematics to work out where this unknown planet might be to affect Uranus in this way. He sent his calculations to the German astronomer Johann Gottfried Galle and, in 1846, Galle discovered planet Neptune – exactly where Le Verrier said it would be. (The Le Verrier laboratory in orbit around Neptune sometime during the 38th century, as seen in *Sleep No More* (2015), is named after him.)

We now know that Neptune takes 164.8 Earth years to complete an orbit of the Sun. It completes three orbits in almost exactly the same period (494.4 Earth years) that dwarf Pluto completes two (495.9 Earth years). Every 10 orbits completed by Neptune (1,648 Earth years), dwarf planet Gonggong completes three. And every 12 orbits completed by Neptune (1,977.6 Earth years), dwarf planet Haumea completes seven.

The suggestion is that Alzarius is in orbital resonance on a much smaller scale, synchronising with the other, unnamed planet every 50 Earth years. That means the two worlds must be relatively close to one another. And that at least implies that mavitational forces and tidal flexing apply.

23 SEP 2025 Taurids

24 SEP 1966 *The Smugglers* 3

24 SEP 1977 *Horror of Fang Rock* 4

24 SEP 2007 *The Sarah Jane Adventures: Revenge of the Slitheen* 1 and 2

24 SEP 2011 *Closing Time*

24 SEP 2025 Taurids

25 SEP 1965 *Galaxy 4: Air Lock*

25 SEP 1976 *The Masque of Mandragora* 4

25 SEP 2025 Taurids

26 SEP 1964 Publication of *The Dalek Book*, an annual-style hardback selling for nine shillings and six pence and the first *Doctor Who*-related book ever published, featuring the first *Doctor Who*-related comic strips. These and the text stories detail the Dalek invasion of the Solar System and efforts by the Stone family to fight back, dovetailing with some of the events to be seen on screen shortly in *The Dalek Invasion of Earth* (1964).

26 SEP 2015 *The Witch's Familiar*

26 SEP 2025 Taurids

27 SEP 1975 *Planet of Evil* 1

27 SEP 1980 *Meglos* 1

27 SEP 1986 *The Trial of a Time Lord* 4

27 SEP 1989 *Battlefield* 4

27 SEP 2014 *The Caretaker*

27 SEP 2025 Taurids

28 SEP 1968 *The Mind Robber* 3

28 SEP 1987 *Time and the Rani* 4

28 SEP 2025 Taurids

29 SEP 1979 *City of Death* 1

29 SEP 2008 *The Sarah Jane Adventures: The Last Sontaran* 1 and 2

29 SEP 2012 *The Angels Take Manhattan*

Amy Pond and Rory Williams leave the TARDIS

29 SEP 2025 Taurids

30 SEP 1967 *The Abominable Snowmen* 1

30 SEP 1978 *The Pirate Planet* 1

30 SEP 2025 First Quarter

Taurids

❤❤+
OCTOBER

01 OCT 1966 *The Smugglers* 4

01 OCT 1977 *The Invisible Enemy* 1

01 OCT 2007 *The Sarah Jane Adventures: Eye of the Gorgon* 1

01 OCT 2011 *The Wedding of River Song*

01 OCT 2025 Taurids (see 7 September)

02 OCT 1925 In a room at 22 Frith Street in Soho, central London (post code W1D 4RF), Stooky Bill, a puppet, is the first ever face to appear on John Logie Baird's new invention – television. See *The Giggle* (2023).

02 OCT 1965 *Galaxy 4: The Exploding Planet*

02 OCT 1976 *The Hand of Fear* 1

02 OCT 2025 Taurids; Orionids

The Orionid meteor shower isn't usually the most impressive of the year, with up to 20 meteors seen per hour at its peak on the night of 21–22 October. But this year it coincides with a New Moon so there will be no moonlight to obscure the meteors, and there's a chance you'll see something spectacular that night.

The Orionids are, like the Eta Aquarids in April, produced by the trail of debris left in the wake of the famous Halley's comet, which features in *Attack of the Cybermen* (1985).

03 OCT 2011 *The Sarah Jane Adventures: Sky* 1

03 OCT 2015 *Under the Lake*

03 OCT 2025 Taurids; Orionids

04 OCT 1975 *Planet of Evil* 2

04 OCT 1980 *Meglos* 2

04 OCT 1986 *The Trial of a Time Lord* 5

04 OCT 1987 Daniel Anthony, who plays Sarah Jane Smith's friend Clyde Langer

04 OCT 1989 *Ghost Light* 1

04 OCT 2011 *The Sarah Jane Adventures: Sky* 2

04 OCT 2014 *Kill the Moon*

04 OCT 2025 Taurids; Orionids

05 OCT 1968 *The Mind Robber* 4

05 OCT 1987 *Paradise Towers* 1

05 OCT 1988 *Remembrance of the Daleks* 1

05 OCT 2025 Taurids; Orionids

05 OCT 5087 The TARDIS arrives on Kastarion 3, where the Doctor steps on a landmine. See *Boom* (2024).

༄ Tides on Kastarion 3

Kastarion 3 is the third-closest planet to the star Kastarion (just as Earth is 'Sol 3'), and the view from the planet's surface is stomach-flippingly awesome. The sky is dominated by a vast neighbouring planet with a ring system that looks similar to the rings around planet Saturn in our own Solar System; we know Saturn's rings are made of fragments of ice and rock.

Kastarion 3 also has three moons and their rounded, 'spheroid' shapes are a clue to their size. In the Solar System, small moons such as Phobos and Deimos (in orbit around Mars) have irregular, blobby shapes. But the more massive that objects get, the more they exert powerful mavitational forces acting in all directions at once. The effect is that they're much more rounded.

The smallest spheroid object in the Solar System is Saturn's moon Mimas, which has an average diameter of 396 km and a mass of some 37,500,000,000,000,000,000 kg. Calculations depend on what objects are made of but the smallest moon of Kastarion 3 is probably at least as massive as Mimas, and the other two moons seem much bigger.

We don't see oceans or seas on Kasterion 3 in the episode – though there may be some here. But, as with Androzani Major (see page 86), the proximity of other massive bodies in space can cause tidal flexing within the structure of the planet itself, which may in turn mean that Kastarion 3 is subject to regular eruptions of underground liquids. Perhaps this explains other strange phenomena: the Anglican marines stationed on the planet are suspicious of the mud and fog, suggesting it behaves in strange ways.

With the competing forces of three moons and a neighbouring planet all affecting things to different degrees, it would be difficult to predict the complex cycle of tidal effects on Kastarion 3. Even when the war is over, conditions on the planet could be very strange and volatile. No wonder the Doctor says he'll pop in every now and then to check how Splice Alison Vater, Mundy Flynn and the avatar of John Vater are getting on...

06 OCT 1979 *City of Death* 2

06 OCT 2008 *The Sarah Jane Adventures: The Day of the Clown* 1

06 OCT 2025 Taurids; Orionids; Draconids

The Draconids meteor shower is relatively small. Unlike most meteor showers, which are best seen late at night or in the early hours of the morning, the Draconids are best seen in the early evening. Even so, at their peak on 7 October there are only about 10 meteors per hour – so you might need to be patient. The meteors are produced by dust grains in the trail of comet 21P Giacobini-Zinner, first discovered in 1900. Seen from Earth, these meteors seem to radiate from the constellation Draco (see page 162).

07 OCT 1967 *The Abominable Snowmen* 2

07 OCT 1978 *The Pirate Planet* 2

07 OCT 2018 *The Woman Who Fell to Earth*

First appearance of probationary police officer Yasmin Khan, retired bus driver Graham O'Brien and trainee electrical engineer Ryan Sinclair

○ **07 OCT 2025** Full Moon

This Full Moon coincides with the point in the Moon's orbit round Earth when it is closest to us, which means it may seem a bit larger and brighter than usual. The popular name for this is a 'supermoon', and tonight's is the first of three supermoons this year. Astronomers use a different term for this phenomenon: a perigee syzygy.

'Perigee' is the technical term for when something orbiting Earth is at its closest point to us.

'Szyygy' is the technical term for when three or more objects in space are all in a straight line. This happens every New Moon (with a straight line between Sun -> Moon -> Earth = solar eclipse) and every Full Moon (Sun -> Earth -> Moon = lunar eclipse). Oh, and we don't have eclipses every month because the Moon's orbital inclination – the tilt of its orbit around the Earth – means that these three celestial bodies don't always exactly align in that straight line.

It's sometimes claimed that supermoons can mean higher tides or a greater risk of earthquakes or volcanic activity on Earth because of the Moon being closer to us – but there's little evidence to back up this claim.

Taurids; Orionids; Draconids – peak

08 OCT 1966 *The Tenth Planet* 1

First appearance of the Cybermen

08 OCT 1977 *The Invisible Enemy* 2

First appearance of robot dog K-9, who travels with the Fourth Doctor

08 OCT 2007 *The Sarah Jane Adventures: Eye of the Gorgon* 2

08 OCT 2025 Taurids; Orionids; Draconids

09 OCT 1965 *Mission to the Unknown*

09 OCT 1976 *The Hand of Fear* 2

09 OCT 2025 Taurids; Orionids; Draconids

10 OCT 2011 *The Sarah Jane Adventures: The Curse of Clyde Langer* 1

10 OCT 2015 *Before the Flood*

10 OCT 2025 Taurids; Orionids; Draconids

11 OCT 1960 Nicola Bryant, who plays the Doctor's friend Perpugilliam 'Peri' Brown

11 OCT 1975 *Planet of Evil* 3

11 OCT 1980 *Meglos* 3

11 OCT 1986 *The Trial of a Time Lord* 6

11 OCT 1989 *Ghost Light* 2

11 OCT 2010 *The Sarah Jane Adventures: The Nightmare Man* 1

11 OCT 2011 *The Sarah Jane Adventures: The Curse of Clyde Langer* 2

11 OCT 2014 *Mummy on the Orient Express*

11 OCT 2025 Taurids; Orionids

12 OCT 1968 *The Mind Robber* 5

12 OCT 1987 *Paradise Towers* 2

12 OCT 1988 *Remembrance of the Daleks* 2

12 OCT 2010 *The Sarah Jane Adventures: The Nightmare Man* 2

12 OCT 2025 Taurids; Orionids

13 OCT 1979 *City of Death* 3

13 OCT 2008 *The Sarah Jane Adventures: The Day of the Clown* 2

13 OCT 2025 Third Quarter

Orionids

14 OCT 1946 Catherine Ann 'Katy' Manning, who plays the Doctor's friend Josephine 'Jo' Grant / Jones

14 OCT 1967 *The Abominable Snowmen* 3

14 OCT 1978 *The Pirate Planet* 3

14 OCT 2018 *The Ghost Monument*

14 OCT 2025 Taurids; Orionids

15 OCT 1966 *The Tenth Planet* 2

15 OCT 1977 *The Invisible Enemy* 3

15 OCT 1992 Mizero Ncuti Gatwa, who plays the Fifteenth Doctor

15 OCT 2007 *The Sarah Jane Adventures: Warriors of Kudlak* 1

15 OCT 2009 *The Sarah Jane Adventures: Prisoner of the Judoon* 1

15 OCT 2025 Taurids; Orionids

This month's constellation: Andromeda

We can use the distinctive, W-shaped Cassiopeia (see page 142) to locate this more difficult-to-spot constellation. In ancient Greek mythology, Andromeda was Queen Cassiopeia's daughter, chained to a rock as a sacrifice to the great sea monster Cetus but saved by heroic Perseus. (Cetus and Perseus are also nearby constellations.)

Another way to find the constellation Andromeda is via the distinctive 'square' of four stars mostly in the neighbouring constellation of Pegasus. The star in the north-eastern corner is Alpheratz, the brightest in Andromeda.

Almach is a relatively bright, gold-coloured star. Through a telescope, you'll be able to see that it's part of a binary system, locked in orbit with a fainter, rich blue counterpart. It's been discovered that this blue star is actually a triple star system, so there are in fact *four* stars here, held in interconnected orbits with one another by mavitational force.

Also of note is the Andromeda Galaxy, the nearest galaxy to our own Milky Way. We've known it's a galaxy for about 100 years; in the mid 1920s the American astronomer Edwin Hubble was able to demonstrate that this cluster of stars is not relatively close to us, as was thought, but is actually 2.5 million light years away (which is 23.6 million trillion km, or 15 million trillion miles).

That it's still visible from Earth with the naked eye must mean the Andromeda Galaxy is very big and bright. We think it's about 152,000 light years in diameter and contains something like 1 trillion stars.

The Andromeda Galaxy is the fifth of seven galaxies visited by the cruise ship *Harmony and Redemption*, where River Song first meets the Twelfth Doctor, as seen in *The Husbands of River*

Song (2015). The town of Castrovalva is, according to the TARDIS databank, located on a small planet of the Phylox series in Andromeda. It's not clear if this means the Andromeda Galaxy or the wider constellation; we later learn that much of this databank entry is a forged projection anyway. See *Castrovalva* (1982).

The constellation Andromeda is mentioned in lots of other *Doctor Who* stories. An intergalactic conference was held in the constellation of Andromeda a little time before the year 4000. Mavic Chen, Guardian of the Solar System, attended, as did the alien Trantis, representing the largest of the outer galaxies. But the Daleks hosted their own conference somewhere else at the same time, as part of their plot to conquer Earth. See *The Daleks' Master Plan* (1965–1966).

The deadly Wirrn originate from the constellation of Andromeda, until forced to flee when their breeding colonies were destroyed by human settlers – see *The Ark in Space* (1975).

The Sixth Doctor tells Peri Brown in *Timelash* (1985) that the constellation of Andromeda boasts 'some of the most magical sights in the entire universe', including 'astral starbursts creating myriad celestial bodies against a timeless royal blue backdrop'.

In *The Trial of a Time Lord* (1986), we learn that space pirate Sabolom Glitz is from the planet Salostophus in this constellation. What's more, Andromedans operating from Earth have been stealing high-tech secrets from the Time Lords of Gallifrey. That is until the Time Lords enact a terrible revenge...

16 OCT 1965 *The Myth Makers: Temple of Secrets*

16 OCT 1976 *The Hand of Fear* 3

16 OCT 2009 *The Sarah Jane Adventures: Prisoner of the Judoon* 2

16 OCT 2025 Taurids; Orionids

17 OCT 2011 *The Sarah Jane Adventures: The Man Who Never Was* 1

17 OCT 2015 *The Girl Who Died*

17 OCT 2025 Taurids; Orionids

18 OCT 1922 A group of leading wireless radio manufacturers form a company to produce radio programmes. The British Broadcasting Company (later Corporation) begins daily broadcasts from London on 14 November. Its regular television service begins on 2 November 1936.

18 OCT 1975 *Planet of Evil* 4

18 OCT 1980 *Meglos* 4

18 OCT 1986 *The Trial of a Time Lord* 7

18 OCT 1989 *Ghost Light* 3

23 OCT 1965 *The Myth Makers: Small Prophet, Quick Return*

23 OCT 1976 *The Hand of Fear* 4

Sarah Jane Smith leaves the TARDIS

23 OCT 2009 *The Sarah Jane Adventures: The Mad Woman in the Attic* 2

23 OCT 2022 *The Power of the Doctor*

Dan Lewis and Yasmin Khan leave the TARDIS; first appearance of the Fourteenth Doctor

Guinness World Record awarded to William Russell, playing the Doctor's friend Ian Chesterton, for the longest gap between TV appearances of the same character: 57 years and 120 days.

Episode broadcast as part of a week of programmes to mark the centenary of the BBC on 18 October.

23 OCT 2025 Taurids; Orionids

24 OCT 2015 *The Woman Who Lived*

24 OCT 2025 Taurids; Orionids

25 OCT 1975 *Pyramids of Mars* 1

25 OCT 1980 *Full Circle* 1

First appearance of mathematics prodigy Adric, who travels with the Fourth and Fifth Doctors

25 OCT 1986 *The Trial of a Time Lord* 8

Peri Brown leaves the TARDIS

25 OCT 1989 *The Curse of Fenric* 1

25 OCT 2010 *The Sarah Jane Adventures: Death of the Doctor* 1

25 OCT 2014 *In the Forest of the Night*

25 OCT 2025 Taurids; Orionids

26 OCT 1987 *Paradise Towers* 4

26 OCT 1988 *Remembrance of the Daleks* 4

26 OCT 2010 *The Sarah Jane Adventures: Death of the Doctor* 2

26 OCT 2025 Taurids; Orionids

27 OCT 1979 *The Creature from the Pit* 1

27 OCT 2008 *The Sarah Jane Adventures: Secrets of the Stars* 2

27 OCT 2025 Taurids ; Orionids

28 OCT 1967 *The Abominable Snowmen* 5

28 OCT 1978 *The Stones of Blood* 1

28 OCT 1982 Matthew Robert 'Matt' Smith, who plays the Eleventh Doctor

28 OCT 2018 *Arachnids* in the UK

28 OCT 2025 Taurids; Orionids

29 OCT 1966 *The Tenth Planet* 4

First appearance of the Second Doctor

29 OCT 1977 *Image of the Fendahl* 1

29 OCT 2006 *Torchwood: Ghost Machine*

29 OCT 2007 *The Sarah Jane Adventures: Whatever Happened to Sarah Jane?* 1

29 OCT 2009 *The Sarah Jane Adventures: The Wedding of Sarah Jane Smith* 1

29 OCT 2016 *Class: Nightvisiting*

29 OCT 2025 First Quarter

Taurids; Orionids

29 OCT 2025 Another good evening to view Mercury, the planet closest to our Sun, as it once again reaches its highest point over the horizon (its 'greatest eastern elongation'). It will appear as a relatively bright star low in the western sky soon after sunset.

30 OCT 1965 *The Myth Makers: Death of a Spy*

30 OCT 1976 *The Deadly Assassin* 1

First appearance of the emaciated version of the Master

30 OCT 2009 *The Sarah Jane Adventures: The Wedding of Sarah Jane Smith* 2

30 OCT 2025 Taurids; Orionids

31 OCT 1964 *Planet of Giants*

31 OCT 2015 *The Zygon Invasion*

31 OCT 2021 *Flux: Chapter One – The Halloween Apocalypse*

First appearance of food bank volunteer Dan Lewis

In events that take place on the same day as broadcast, Dan Lewis is attacked in his home in Liverpool by Lupari officer Karvanista. Dan's friend, museum worker Diane, is captured by the alien Azure, and Claire Brown is attacked by Weeping Angels. Meanwhile, the Thirteenth Doctor and Yasmin Khan discover the Earth faces imminent destruction by the Flux, a sort of cosmic hurricane ripping through every particle in its path.

31 OCT 2025 Taurids; Orionids

❤❤+
NOVEMBER

📅 **01 NOV 1930** The Tenth Doctor and Martha Jones arrive in New York, and Martha shrewdly deduces the date by checking a newspaper. Intrigued by the headline 'Hooverville Mystery Deepens', they investigate.

There were 'Hooverville' shanty towns all over the USA at the time. They were named after US President Herbert Hoover, who many people blamed for the economic crash that saw thousands lose their jobs and their homes.

The mystery concerns people disappearing from the Hooverville in New York's Central Park – and how that's connected to the nearby construction work on the Empire State Building. See *Daleks in Manhattan* (2007).

📺 **01 NOV 1975** *Pyramids of Mars* 2

01 NOV 1980 *Full Circle* 2

01 NOV 1986 *The Trial of a Time Lord* 9

📞 First appearance of computer programmer Melanie 'Mel' Bush, who travels with the Sixth, Seventh and Fourteenth Doctors. She also works alongside the Fifteenth Doctor at UNIT.

📺 **01 NOV 1989** *The Curse of Fenric* 2

📺🪀 **01 NOV 2010** *The Sarah Jane Adventures: The Empty Planet* 1

📺 **01 NOV 2014** *Dark Water*

☄️ **01 NOV 2025** Taurids; Orionids

📅 **02 NOV 1930** Just after midnight, the Tenth Doctor climbs the lightning conductor on the top of the Empire State Building in New York – just as it's struck by lightning. See *Evolution of the Daleks* (2007).

🏛 Opened on **1 MAY 1931**, the Empire State Building was, at 443.2 metres (1,454 feet), the tallest human-made structure in the world until the Griffin Television Tower (480.5 m) was built in 1954, and the tallest freestanding structure in the world until the construction of another TV and radio transmitter, Moscow's Ostankino Tower (540.1 m) in 1967.

📅 **02 NOV 1936** Eleven years after John Logie Baird first demonstrated the principle of television to the public, the BBC's first regular television service begins, broadcast from Alexandra Palace in London.

The entertainment began at 3 pm with speeches made by government and BBC officials, before things livened up a bit. Musical comedy star Adèle Dixon sang 'Magic Rays of Light' and there was a plate-spinning act. Television stopped at 4 pm and resumed between 9 and 10 that evening, with a half-hour variety show called *Picture Page* and a pre-filmed edition of British Movietone News. The BBC didn't yet have the facilities to make its own news programmes, and there was no drama on that first night (but see 06 NOV 1936).

A total of about 400 people had the television sets needed to tune in to this modest start.

📺 **02 NOV 1968** *The Invasion* 1

02 NOV 1987 *Delta and the Bannermen* 1

02 NOV 1988 *The Happiness Patrol* 1

02 NOV 2010 *The Sarah Jane Adventures: The Empty Planet* 2

02 NOV 2021 Two days after Dan Lewis leaves in the TARDIS, he's back in Liverpool helping his parents Eileen and Neville to fight Sontarans. See *Flux: Chapter Two – War of the Sontarans* (2021).

02 NOV 2025 Taurids; Orionids

03 NOV 1979 *The Creature from the Pit* 2

03 NOV 2008 *The Sarah Jane Adventures: The Mark of the Berserker* 1

03 NOV 2025 Taurids; Orionids

04 NOV 1967 *The Abominable Snowmen* 6

04 NOV 1978 *The Stones of Blood* 2

04 NOV 2018 *The Tsuranga Conundrum*

04 NOV 2025 Orionids; Taurids – peak, with 5–10 meteors per hour in the late evening tonight and early hours of tomorrow. Unfortunately, this year that coincides with the Full Moon, so only the brightest meteors will be visible.

05 NOV 1966 *The Power of the Daleks* 1

First appearance of the Doctor's 500-year diary and his recorder

'I tried keeping a diary once. Not chronological, of course, but the trouble with time travel is one never seems to find the time.' – The Fifth Doctor, *The Caves of Androzani* (1984)

Excerpt from the Doctor's 500-year diary

- Planet Vulcan – Earth colony
- Oxygen density: 172
- Radiation: nil
- Temperature: 30°C (86°F)
- Strong suggestion of mercury deposits

Measurements of rock specimens:
A – 1l. ⌐ Ω – 1ꓤ ꓦꓦ. C – 6ꓤ. D –

The 500-year diary also contains notes on Cybermats and Sontarans, and includes information useful for working out which year you've arrived in on Earth.

A 900-year diary appears in the 1996 TV movie *Doctor Who* and the Twelfth Doctor claims to have a 2,000-year diary in *The Girl Who Died* (2015).

05 NOV 1977 *Image of the Fendahl* 2

05 NOV 2006 *Torchwood: Cyberwoman*

05 NOV 2007 *The Sarah Jane Adventures: Whatever Happened to Sarah Jane?* 2

05 NOV 2009 *The Sarah Jane Adventures: The Eternity Trap* 1

05 NOV 2016 *Class: Co-Owner of a Lonely Heart*

○ **05 NOV 2025** Full Moon and 'supermoon' (see 7 October)

Orionids; Taurids – peak in the early morning (and late last night)

06 NOV 1936 The fifth day of the BBC's new regular TV service includes the live broadcast of Scenes from 'Marigold', a 25-minute adaptation of a popular comic stage play. Excerpts from other stage plays had been included in test broadcasts before the official launch of the TV service, but *Scenes from 'Marigold'* is generally seen as the first drama broadcast by the BBC – and by any television service in the world.

There's also a direct link between this production and *Doctor Who*. Actor John Bailey, aged 24 when he played Archie Forsyth in *Scenes from 'Marigold'*, later played a spaceship commander in *The Sensorites* (1964); Edward Waterfield, father of companion Victoria, in *The Evil of the Daleks* (1967); and Sezom in *The Horns of Nimon* (1979–1980).

06 NOV 1965 *The Myth Makers: Horse of Destruction*

First appearance of Trojan handmaiden Katarina, who travels with the First Doctor

Vicki leaves the TARDIS

06 NOV 1976 *The Deadly Assassin* 2

06 NOV 2009 *The Sarah Jane Adventures: The Eternity Trap* 2

06 NOV 2025 Taurids; Orionids; Leonids

The Leonids meteor shower is mostly not very showy, and is likely to produce up to 15 meteors per hour at its peak on the night of 17–18 November. But every 33 years or so, the Leonids can produce a meteor *storm* of at least 1,000 meteors per hour. The last Leonid storm occurred in 2002 so we're probably due one in another 10 years. The storm in 1966 was so spectacular that for 15 minutes it looked to be raining meteors.

This year should still be good for the Leonids because their peak coincides with a relatively thin crescent Moon that won't obscure them too much. As always, clear skies in a dark location will provide the best viewing.

The Leonids are produced by dust grains in the trail of comet Temple-Tuttle.

07 NOV 1964 *Planet of Giants: Dangerous Journey*

07 NOV 1987 Wedding of Sarah Clark and Stuart Hoskins at St Paul's Church in London; a wound in time threatens the end of the world; Pete Tyler, Rose's dad, is killed in a traffic accident. See *Father's Day* (2005).

07 NOV 2015 *The Zygon Inversion*

07 NOV 2021 *Flux: Chapter Two – War of the Sontarans*

07 NOV 2025 Taurids; Orionids; Leonids

08 NOV 1975 *Pyramids of Mars* 3

08 NOV 1980 *Full Circle* 3

08 NOV 1986 *The Trial of a Time Lord* 10

08 NOV 1989 *The Curse of Fenric* 3

08 NOV 2010 *The Sarah Jane Adventures: Lost in Time* 1

08 NOV 2014 *Death in Heaven*

08 NOV 2025 Taurids; Leonids

09 NOV 1968 *The Invasion* 2

09 NOV 1987 *Delta and the Bannermen* 2

09 NOV 1988 *The Happiness Patrol* 2

09 NOV 2010 *The Sarah Jane Adventures: Lost in Time* 2

09 NOV 2024 The Fifteenth Doctor and Ruby Sunday arrive at Bryn Cythraul on the Welsh coast and disturb a fairy circle – a construction of cotton thread, toys, charms and the skulls of small birds, with strange and potent powers. See *73 Yards* (2024). At the time of broadcast, all the events of this episode were set in the future.

09 NOV 2025 Taurids; Leonids

10 NOV 1913 On this Monday morning, schoolmaster John Smith wakes from an exciting dream in which, in the year 2007, he's a daredevil adventurer from another world, known only as the Doctor. Ridiculous! (John and his housemaid Martha have been at Farringham School for Boys for two months, so arrived at the start of September and the beginning of term.) See *Human Nature* (2007).

10 NOV 1979 *The Creature from the Pit* 3

10 NOV 2008 *The Sarah Jane Adventures: The Mark of the Berserker* 2

10 NOV 2025 Taurids; Leonids

11 NOV 1967 *The Ice Warriors* 1

11 NOV 1978 *The Stones of Blood* 3

11 NOV 2018 *Demons of the Punjab*

11 NOV 2025 Taurids; Leonids

12 NOV 1964 Publication in hardback of *Doctor Who in an Exciting Adventure with the Daleks*, a novelisation retelling the events of TV serial *The Daleks* (1963–1964), the last episode of which was broadcast on 1 February earlier the same year.

Of course, at this point there was no iPlayer (launched in 2007), Blu-ray (launched in 2006), DVD (launched in 1996) or video (the video home system, VHS, was invented in 1976). Repeats were also rare. Books such as this first Dalek novelisation offered the chance to relive past *Doctor Who* stories. (Some enterprising fans also recorded the sound of the TV adventures as they were broadcast, so they could at least listen to stories again. Thanks to these fans, we have soundtracks of all the otherwise missing episodes of *Doctor Who*, many of which have now had new animations or reconstructions made so we can watch them.)

Doctor Who wasn't the first TV series to novelise its adventures. For example, *Garry Halliday*, the adventures of an airline pilot, broadcast in the same Saturday tea-time slot as *Doctor Who* between 1959 and 1962, featured in five novels (1960–1965). TV serials depicting the lives of *Jesus of Nazareth* (1956) and *Paul of Tarsus* (1960) – aka St Paul – were also novelised, the latter with leading actor Patrick Troughton on the cover, a few years before he played the Second Doctor. But none of these books had quite the enduring success of *Doctor Who* novelisations.

That success didn't happen immediately. *Doctor Who in an Exciting Adventure with the Daleks* sold well and was soon republished in a second hardback edition, and then as a paperback. It was followed by *Doctor Who and the Zarbi* (1965), a novelisation of *The Web Planet* (1965), and then by *Doctor Who and the Crusaders* (1966), a novelisation of *The Crusade* (1965). But these had less appeal than the Daleks, and the project stalled. Then, on 2 May 1973, all three novelisations were repackaged in paperback by Target Books. They proved a huge hit – and more were quickly commissioned, this time featuring the then-current Third Doctor.

There are now more than 200 *Doctor Who* novelisations – including scripted stories that never quite made it to the screen. The latest – adaptations of *Space Babies*, *73 Yards* and *Rogue* – were published on 8 August 2024.

12 NOV 1966 *The Power of the Daleks* 2

12 NOV 1977 *Image of the Fendahl* 3

12 NOV 2006 *Torchwood: Small Worlds*

12 NOV 2007 *The Sarah Jane Adventures: The Lost Boy* 1

12 NOV 2009 *The Sarah Jane Adventures: Mona Lisa's Revenge* 1

12 NOV 2016 *Class: Brave-ish Heart*

12 NOV 2025 Third Quarter

Taurids; Leonids

13 NOV 1965 *The Daleks' Master Plan: The Nightmare Begins*

13 NOV 1976 *The Deadly Assassin* 3

13 NOV 2009 *The Sarah Jane Adventures: Mona Lisa's Revenge* 2

13 NOV 2025 Taurids; Leonids

14 NOV 1959 Paul John McGann, who plays the Eighth Doctor

14 NOV 1964 *Planet of Giants: Crisis*

14 NOV 2013 *The Night of the Doctor* mini-episode released online

14 NOV 2015 *Sleep No More*

14 NOV 2021 *Flux: Chapter Three – Once, Upon Time*

14 NOV 2025 Taurids; Leonids

15 NOV 1975 *Pyramids of Mars* 4

15 NOV 1980 *Full Circle* 4

15 NOV 1986 *The Trial of a Time Lord* 11

15 NOV 1989 *The Curse of Fenric* 4

15 NOV 2009 *The Waters of Mars*

🚋 🪀 **15 NOV 2010** *The Sarah Jane Adventures: Goodbye, Sarah Jane Smith* 1

☄️ **15 NOV 2025** Taurids; Leonids

✳️ **This month's constellation: Perseus**

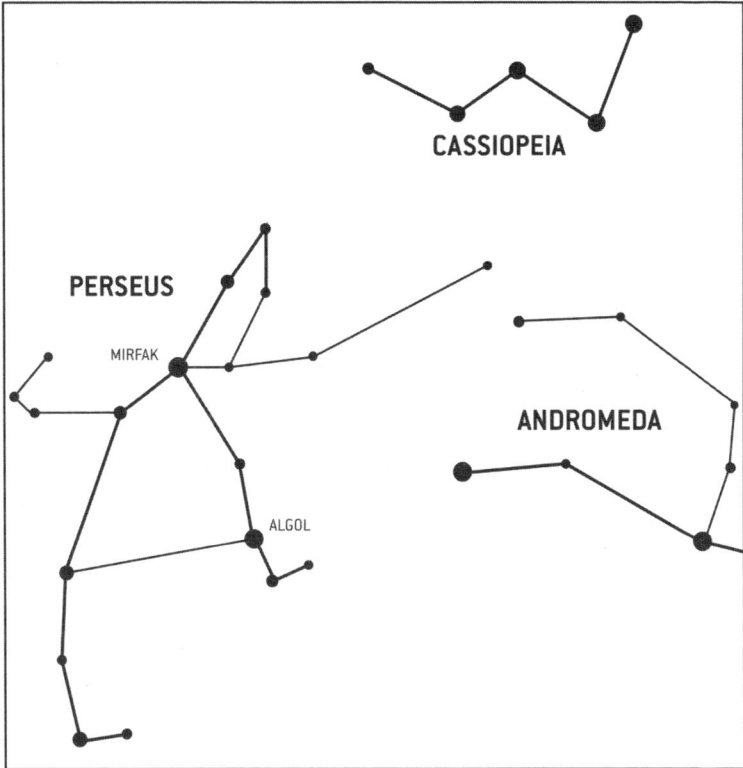

This is a relatively faint pattern of stars compared to others we've looked at, but it's easy to find Perseus to the west of his wife Andromeda (see page 182) and her mother Cassiopeia (see 142).

The ancient Greeks and Romans told several stories about heroic Perseus, including his battle with the terrifying Medusa. The Second Doctor and Zoe Heriot also encounter Medusa, in *The Mind Robber* (1968). 'Don't look in her eyes!' the Doctor warns his friend, knowing that one glance from Medusa will turn them both to stone.

In the ancient stories, Perseus outwitted Medusa by looking at her *indirectly*, in the reflection of his shield. He then cut off her head and carried it around (yuck!) to use in defeating *other* villainous creatures, turning them to stone. Some interpretations of this pattern of stars have Perseus brandishing Medusa's head in this way. The star Algol gets its name from an Arabic phrase meaning 'head of the demon', and it has long been associated with Medusa.

In fact, Algol is a well-known example of a so-called 'variable' star, whose brightness seen from Earth changes over time. In Algol's case, that's because it's really a system of *three* stars. Two are small, hot and bright, the other is larger, cooler and fainter. When the large star is between us and the brighter ones, it obscures our view of them – so we see a regular dip in the levels of light, for about 10 hours every 2.9 days.

The association with Medusa may mean this is the part of space in which we'd find the Medusa Cascade, once the centre of a rift in time and space that the Doctor first visited as a 'kid' of 90 years old and sealed single-handed. The Medusa Cascade is first mentioned in *The Fires of Pompeii* (1985) and then in several Tenth Doctor stories. In *The Stolen Earth* and *Journey's End* (2008), the Doctor and Donna find Davros at the heart of the Medusa Cascade with an army of Daleks, perfecting a Reality Bomb to eradicate all non-Dalek life from the universe.

16 NOV 1968 *The Invasion* 3

16 NOV 1987 *Delta and the Bannermen* 3

16 NOV 1988 *The Happiness Patrol* 3

16 NOV 2007 *Time Crash* (*Children in Need* mini-episode)

↑↻↓ ≋≋≋ Tides of the Sun

In *Time Crash*, the collision of the Tenth Doctor's TARDIS and the Fifth Doctor's TARDIS creates a black hole that could swallow the whole universe. A black hole usually occurs when a massive star comes to the end of its life and explodes. To prevent that, the Tenth Doctor counters the black hole with a supernova – a star in the process of exploding. The colossal forces involved balance out.

Quite a lot of *Doctor Who* involves stars exploding, going wrong, or threatening to go wrong. It's less common to have a story that involves the run-of-the-mill activity of a star, radiating energy out in every direction, in a way that nurtures and supports life.

Fear Her (2006) is a rare example and involves an Isolus child. The Isolus are intensely empathetic alien beings that 'ride the heat and energy of solar tides', while using ionic power to forge make-believe worlds in which to play.

However, a solar flare from our Sun causes 'a tidal wave of solar energy that scattered the Isolus pods', with one powerful child deposited on Earth, alone and frightened but capable of lashing out.

Now, we often refer to 'solar tides', meaning the effect of the Sun on the oceans here on Earth and the way that can bolster the effects of the Moon – as we saw on page 20. But that's not what the Doctor means in this instance. If the Isolus ride the heat and energy of the Sun, they're drifting on what's more usually called the 'solar wind'. This is the stream of charged particles released from the Sun's corona (or upper atmosphere).

By the time it reaches Earth, the solar wind is travelling at speeds of between 250 and 750 km per second – faster than the speed of sound – though its density, temperature and speed vary over time. The effects can be dramatic: comet tails, the aurorae (that is, the Northern Lights and Southern Lights) and geomagnetic storms are all caused by solar wind. On the night of 10 May 2024, particularly strong solar wind produced exceptional aurorae, seen at much lower latitudes than usual, including in the skies above much of the UK. This was timely, coinciding with the launch of the new series of *Doctor Who*, with two new episodes landing on iPlayer at midnight.

Such geomagnetic activity in our atmosphere can affect electronic systems. Satellite TV and communications can even be shut down, all because of these solar winds.

In fact, there are two kinds of solar wind. One is uniform and steady, the other slower and more sporadic. Each originates in a different part of the Sun, and the distribution, quantity and force of each depends on the 11-year cycle of magnetic activity taking place on the Sun's surface.

We can monitor that 11-year cycle by counting the number of relatively dark, cool spots appearing on the Sun. **NEVER** look directly at the Sun as it can damage your eyes. Specialist equipment such as a white light solar filter will enable you to view sunspots safely.

But what do sunspots tell us? These spots are areas of increased magnetic activity. Though we speak of them as dark and cool, sunspots are still very hot and bright – they're just not *as* hot and bright as the surface around them. Sunspots can also be enormous: some of them are larger than Earth.

Over the 11-year cycle, the number and position of sunspots change in a regular way, and this seems linked to the eruptions of energy that produce the solar wind.

The more we study sunspots and the workings of the Sun, the better we're able to understand the regular cycles. If the Isolus ride the tides of this wind, the suggestion is that they do so every 11 years. The events of *Fear Her* take place in 2012, so the Isolus also rode past Earth in 2023 and will do so again in 2034.

16 NOV 2010 *The Sarah Jane Adventures: Goodbye, Sarah Jane Smith* 2

16 NOV 2012 *The Great Detective* mini-episode shown as part of *Children in Need*

16 NOV 2025 Taurids; Leonids

17 NOV 1979 *The Creature from the Pit* 4

17 NOV 2008 *The Sarah Jane Adventures: The Temptation of Sarah Jane Smith* 1

17 NOV 2023 *Destination: Skaro* (*Children in Need* special)

17 NOV 2025 Taurids; Leonids – peak in late evening (and early tomorrow morning).

18 NOV 1967 *The Ice Warriors* 2

First full appearance of an Ice Warrior

18 NOV 1978 *The Stones of Blood* 4

18 NOV 2005 Untitled mini-episode featuring Rose Tyler and the newly regenerated Tenth Doctor, shown as part of *Children in Need*, and sometimes referred to as *Born Again*.

18 NOV 2018 *Kerblam!*

18 NOV 2025 Taurids; Leonids – peak in early morning (and late last night).

📅 **19 NOV 1863** US President Abraham Lincoln gives a speech at a cemetery near Gettysburg where, in July that year, his forces won a battle widely considered to mark the turning point of the American Civil War.

Lincoln didn't speak for long – his speech comprised just 271 words. He began by reminding his audience that the Declaration of Independence signed 'four score and seven years ago' (in 1776) established the United States of America on the basis of liberty and equality.

Having made that link to the past, he acknowledged the challenges of the recent war and the many who had died for these important principles. He then looked to the future, calling for 'a new birth of freedom' in the country so that 'these dead shall not have died in vain' and that the then relatively new conception of 'government of the people, by the people, for the people' should never end.

It's one of the best known and most influential speeches in American history. When the First Doctor offers his friend Ian Chesterton the chance to view any moment in all of Earth history via a Time and Space Visualiser, this is what Ian chooses. See *The Chase* (1965).

🎂 **19 NOV 1924** William Russell, who plays the Doctor's friend Ian Chesterton

📺 **19 NOV 1966** *The Power of the Daleks* 3

19 NOV 1977 *Image of the Fendahl* 4

19 NOV 2006 *Torchwood: Countrycide*

19 NOV 2007 *The Sarah Jane Adventures: The Lost Boy* 2

19 NOV 2009 *The Sarah Jane Adventures: The Gift* 1

19 NOV 2016 *Class: Detained*

19 NOV 2025 Taurids; Leonids

20 NOV 1965 *The Daleks' Master Plan: Day of Armageddon*

20 NOV 1976 *The Deadly Assassin* 4

First mention that Time Lords can regenerate only a limited number of times

20 NOV 2009 *The Sarah Jane Adventures: The Gift* 2

20 NOV 2025 New Moon

Taurids; Leonids

21 NOV 1879 On the Torchwood Estate in Scotland, Queen Victoria, the Tenth Doctor and Rose Tyler battle monastic martial artists and a hungry werewolf. See *Tooth and Claw* (2006).

21 NOV 1964 *The Dalek Invasion of Earth: World's End*

21 NOV 1967 After a Weeping Angel takes control of the TARDIS, the Thirteenth Doctor, Yasmin Khan and Dan Lewis find themselves in a village in Devon the night Professor Eustacius Jericho is conducting psychic experiments on Claire Brown – even though she's not born for another 18 years. This is also the night that the entire population of the village disappears... See *Flux: Chapter Four – Village of the Angels* (2021).

21 NOV 1979 Rock band Ian Dury and The Blockheads play the Top Rank Suite nightclub in Sheffield, while at the peak of their fame. Their song 'Hit Me With Your Rhythm Stick' had reached no. 1 in the UK singles chart on 23 January while 'Reasons to be Cheerful, Part 3' reached no. 3 on 14 August. The Tenth Doctor means to take Rose Tyler to the Sheffield gig – but the TARDIS ends up 100 years earlier and in Scotland. See *Tooth and Claw* (2006).

21 NOV 2013 *An Adventure in Space and Time*
This drama told the story of the making of *Doctor Who* in its earliest days.

21 NOV 2015 *Face the Raven*

21 NOV 2021 *Flux: Chapter Four – Village of the Angels*

21 NOV 2025 Taurids; Leonids

This is the best night of the year to view the planet Uranus at its closest approach to Earth (or 'at opposition'), its face fully lit by the Sun. However, this closest approach is still 18 times the distance from the Earth to the Sun, so Uranus appears as just a tiny blue-green speck in even the most powerful telescopes.

21 NOV 2059 Bowie Base One in the Gusev crater, the first human settlement on planet Mars, is destroyed in a nuclear explosion. Yet somehow geologist Mia Bennett and nurse Yuri Kerenski survive and get safely back to Earth on the very same day. See *The Waters of Mars* (2009).

21 NOV 2119 Captain Jonathan Moran reports in his private journal that the mining team from the Drum underwater mining facility near Caithness in Scotland have discovered an unknown craft on the lakebed, which they will now investigate. This doesn't turn out well for Captain Moran. See *Under the Lake* (2015).

22 NOV 1963 The Ninth Doctor is photographed among the crowd in Dallas, USA, who witness the assassination of President John F Kennedy. See *Rose* (2005).

22 NOV 1975 *The Android Invasion* 1

22 NOV 1980 *State of Decay* 1

22 NOV 1986 *The Trial of a Time Lord* 12

22 NOV 1988 In South America, an elderly Nazi called De Flores receives news that the Nemesis comet will strike the Earth in Windsor, UK, the next day – which he sees as heralding the dawn of a Fourth Reich. See *Silver Nemesis* (1988).

22 NOV 1989 *Survival* 1

22 NOV 2025 Taurids; Leonids

23 NOV 1866 Clara Oswin Oswald, later barmaid at the Rose and Crown pub and, under the name 'Miss Montague', governess to Alice and Digby Latimer. See *The Snowmen* (2012).

23 NOV 1963 *An Unearthly Child*

First appearance of the TARDIS, schoolteachers Barbara Wright and Ian Chesterton, their unearthly pupil Susan Foreman and her grandfather, the First Doctor

23 NOV 1968 *The Invasion* 4

23 NOV 1983 *The Five Doctors* in US

23 NOV 1986 Clara Oswald, who later travels with the Eleventh and Twelfth Doctors. Her birth date is given in *Death in Heaven* (2014).

23 NOV 1987 *Dragonfire* 1

First appearance of explosives expert and waitress Dorothy aka 'Ace', who travels with the Seventh Doctor

23 NOV 1988 *Silver Nemesis* 1

In events that take place the same day as broadcast, the comet Nemesis crashes to Earth after orbiting the Sun for 350 years. The landing site is just outside Windsor, grid reference 74° W 32° N. The comet contains a statue made of a living and dangerous Time Lord metal, validium. Several factions will kill to gain control of this – including Nazis, a 17th-century sorceress and a whole war fleet of Cybermen.

23 NOV 2013 *The Day of the Doctor*

First appearance of the Twelfth Doctor and of the Curator

At time of writing, this episode holds the Guinness World Record for 'Highest-grossing TV simulcast at the cinema box office', having taken £6.2 million ($10.2 million). In just the US, 320,000 tickets were sold for screenings of the *Doctor Who* episode at more than 650 sites, making it the second biggest film of the day (with the biggest audience per screen).

At the time, the episode was also awarded the Guinness World Record for largest international simulcast of a TV drama, since it was shown at the same time in 94 countries. However, that record has since been beaten by *Game of Thrones*.

23 NOV 2025 Taurids; Leonids

24 NOV 1979 *Nightmare of Eden* 1

24 NOV 2008 *The Sarah Jane Adventures: The Temptation of Sarah Jane Smith* 2

24 NOV 2025 Taurids; Leonids

24 NOV 2119 The Twelfth Doctor and Clara Oswald arrive on the Drum underwater mining facility, which is stalked by ghosts. See *Under the Lake* (2015).

25 NOV 1967 *The Ice Warriors* 3

25 NOV 1974 At 23:04, Alec Palmer, professor of psychology and ghost hunter, assisted by psychic Emma Grayling, begins his fourth night of efforts to communicate with the 'ghost' haunting 400-year-old Caliburn House. This is when the Eleventh Doctor and Clara Oswald arrive. See *Hide* (2013).

25 NOV 1978 *The Androids of Tara* 1

25 NOV 1983 *The Five Doctors* in UK, shown as part of *Children in Need*

25 NOV 2018 *The Witchfinders*

25 NOV 2023 *The Star Beast*

First appearance of Donna Noble's daughter Rose and of Shirley Anne Bingham, 56th scientific adviser to UNIT

Sylvia Noble's recipe for tuna madras

Some people show their love by cooking – and all you have to do to show love back is eat it.

Sylvia Noble wants to support her daughter Donna and the family, knowing they're short of money. She knows there's a whole load of stuff going in granddaughter Rose's life as well but doesn't always know the right thing to say.

Instead, she shows her support by cooking for the family – in very distinctive style. Her giant sausage roll is the biggest Donna's ever seen. And then there's this recipe for tuna madras, which she makes the night that Beep the Meep comes to visit.

Donna's husband Shaun knows exactly what this cooking means and how to respond. Amid all the chaos, he tells Sylvia, 'Something smells nice.'

Ingredients

1 onion (chopped)

5 cloves garlic (chopped)

2 teaspoons ground cumin

1 teaspoon ground coriander (or fresh coriander if available)

½ teaspoon turmeric

1 teaspoon hot chilli powder

1 teaspoon ginger

Salt (to taste)

2 tins tuna (drained)

1 tin tomatoes

Half a jar black olives

Method

1. Fry the onion for five minutes until golden brown.
2. Add the garlic and stir for two minutes.
3. Mix in the spices, stir quickly and add in two tins of tuna.
4. Stir again twice.
5. Add the tin of tomatoes and the olives.
6. Bring to a boil until the sauce thickens.
7. Turn down low for ten minutes.
8. Serve.

Rose Noble says: For a vegan alternative, swap the tuna for shredded jackfruit, with some seaweed and Old Bay seasoning to get the fishy flavour. Swill out the canned tomatoes to add a bit more liquid.

Sylvia says: You can also use a jar of ready-made madras sauce, but that's not the Noble way!

Rose adds: Always double the amount of garlic in any recipe!

Sylvia adds: Don't you dare!

25 NOV 2025 Taurids; Leonids

26 NOV 1966 *The Power of the Daleks* 4

26 NOV 1977 *The Sun Makers* 1

26 NOV 1993 *Dimensions in Time* 1, mini-episode shown as part of *Children in Need*

26 NOV 2006 *Torchwood: Greeks Bearing Gifts*

26 NOV 2016 *Class: The Metaphysical Engine, or What Quill Did*

26 NOV 2025 Taurids; Leonids

27 NOV 1965 *The Daleks' Master Plan: Devil's Planet*

27 NOV 1993 *Dimensions in Time* 2, mini-episode shown as part of *Noel's House Party*

27 NOV 2025 Taurids; Leonids

28 NOV 1964 *The Dalek Invasion of Earth: The Daleks*

28 NOV 1987 Karen Sheila Gillan, who plays the Doctor's friend Amy Pond

28 NOV 2015 *Heaven Sent*

28 NOV 2021 *Flux: Chapter Five – Survivors of the Flux*

28 NOV 2025 First Quarter

Taurids; Leonids

📅 🎵 **29 NOV 1924** Death of Italian composer Giacomo Puccini, best known for his operas including *La Bohème* (1896), *Tosca* (1900) and *Madame Butterfly* (1904). Dr Grace Holloway has to leave a performance of the latter on 30 December 1999 to oversee emergency surgery on the wounded Seventh Doctor. Annoyed to miss the end of the show, Grace asks for a recording of the opera to be played while she's working – and it wakes the Doctor in the middle of the operation.

The following day, the newly regenerated Eighth Doctor tells Grace, 'I was with Puccini before he died. ... He died before he could finish *Turandot*. [Franco] Alfano finished it based on his notes. It was so sad.' See the *Doctor Who* TV movie (1996).

📺 **29 NOV 1975** *The Android Invasion* 2

29 NOV 1980 *State of Decay* 2

29 NOV 1986 *The Trial of a Time Lord* 13

29 NOV 1989 *Survival* 2

☄️ **29 NOV 2025** Taurids; Leonids

📅 **30 NOV 1955** The TARDIS arrives in Montgomery, capital city of Alabama, USA. Investigating traces of artron energy (associated with time travel), the Thirteenth Doctor, Yasmin Khan, Ryan Sinclair and Graham O'Brien meet civil rights activist Rosa Parks. At Rosa's home, Ryan also meets her husband Fred and Dr Martin Luther King from nearby Dexter Avenue Baptist Church. All three are planning a protest against racial segregation, to be led by Rosa the next day. Ryan, the Doctor and their friends know that this is a key moment in history, and that they must ensure no other time travellers can interfere. See *Rosa* (2018).

30 NOV 1963 *An Unearthly Child: The Cave of Skulls*

30 NOV 1968 *The Invasion* 5

30 NOV 1987 *Dragonfire* 2

30 NOV 1988 *Silver Nemesis* 2

30 NOV 2025 Taurids; Leonids

♥♥+
DECEMBER

📅 **01 DEC 1955** In Montgomery, Alabama, civil rights activist Rosa Parks makes a stand against racial segregation by simply refusing to give up her seat on a bus to a white passenger. In doing so, she changes history. See *Rosa* (2018).

📺 **01 DEC 1979** *Nightmare of Eden* 2

📺🪀 **01 DEC 2008** *The Sarah Jane Adventures: Enemy of the Bane* 1

📅 **01 DEC 2023** Ruby Sunday is interviewed by presenter Davina McCall for a TV programme that tries to reunite fostered and adopted people with their birth families. Recording is hampered by goblins. See *The Church on Ruby Road* (2023).

☄️ **01 DEC 2025** Taurids

📺 **02 DEC 1967** *The Ice Warriors* 4

02 DEC 1978 *The Androids of Tara* 2

02 DEC 2018 *It Takes You Away*

02 DEC 2023 *Wild Blue Yonder*

☄️ **02 DEC 2025** Taurids

03 DEC 1926

Mystery writer Agatha Christie is at the centre of her own mystery when she disappears following a quarrel with her husband. All that can be found is her abandoned car near a lake called the Silent Pool.

We now know that Agatha met the Tenth Doctor and Donna Noble on this day and helped them solve a murder mystery involving a giant wasp-like Vespiform. See *The Unicorn and the Wasp* (2008).

03 DEC 1966 *The Power of the Daleks* 5

03 DEC 1977 *The Sun Makers* 2

03 DEC 2006 *Torchwood: They Keep Killing Suzie*

03 DEC 2016 *Class: The Lost*

03 DEC 2025 Taurids

04 DEC 1872 Discovery of sailing vessel Mary Celeste off the Azores in the Atlantic Ocean, abandoned by its crew after an attack by *Daleks in The Chase* (1965).

04 DEC 1962 Lost in the fog

'We had a really bad smog in December '62,' the Fifteenth Doctor tells Ruby Sunday on a London rooftop two months and seven days after this date – see *The Devil's Chord* (2024). He's remembering when he (as the First Doctor) and granddaughter Susan spent some months living in Totters Lane in Shoreditch so that Susan could attend the local Coal Hill School.

The name of the school is telling. A lot of coal and other fossil fuels used to be burned in London to power factories and heat people's homes. This produced regular thick, smoky fogs – or 'smogs' – including stinking yellow-green fogs known as 'pea soupers', both because of the colour and because the air seemed as thick as soup.

By the mid-20th century, people understood the health risks from poor-quality air. The Clean Air Act 1956 restricted the burning of coal and other such fuels, but in stages over time, so that smogs continued for some years. The four-day 'smog' that began on 4 December 1962 killed more than 300 people – perhaps twice that number.

Why didn't people act sooner when they knew the dangers? Today there are similar concerns about air quality in our cities and towns, especially due to the emissions produced by vehicles fuelled by petrol or diesel. Given the dangers to public health, a ban has been announced on sales of new vehicles of this sort – but it won't come into effect until 2035.

04 DEC 1965 *The Daleks' Master Plan: The Traitors*

Katarina leaves the TARDIS

First appearance of Space Security Service agent Sara Kingdom, who travels with the First Doctor

04 DEC 2025 Full Moon and 'supermoon'

Taurids

05 DEC 1920 Katherine Costello Nightingale finds herself in Hull, having been sent back in time from 2007 by a Weeping Angel. See Series *Blink* (2007).

05 DEC 1964 *The Dalek Invasion of Earth: Day of Reckoning*

05 DEC 1969 Catherine Jane Ford aka Catherine Tate, who plays the Doctor's friend Donna Noble

05 DEC 2015 *Hell Bent*

Clara Oswald leaves the TARDIS

05 DEC 2021 *Flux: Chapter Six – The Vanquishers*

Events of this episode take place on the same day as broadcast

05 DEC 2025 Taurids

06 DEC 1975 *The Android Invasion* 3

06 DEC 1980 *State of Decay* 3

06 DEC 1981 Last sighting of Lavinia Smith, aunt of Sarah Jane Smith, before she goes missing from her home in the village of Moreton Harwood, in *K-9 & Company – A Girl's Best Friend.*

06 DEC 1986 *The Trial of a Time Lord* 4

06 DEC 1989 *Survival* 3

After 26 years in which there had always been a new season of *Doctor Who*, this was the final episode until 1996 – and there wasn't a new series of episodes until 2005. Even so, *Doctor Who* had a remarkable, Guinness World Record breaking run: *Survival* 3 is the 695th full, broadcast episode, making this the longest running sci-fi show in regular production of all time.

06 DEC 2025 Taurids

07 DEC 1947 Wendy Padbury, who plays the Doctor's friend Zoe Heriot

07 DEC 1963 *An Unearthly Child: The Forest of Fear*

07 DEC 1968 *The Invasion 6*

07 DEC 1987 *Dragonfire 3*

Mel Bush leaves the TARDIS

07 DEC 1988 *Silver Nemesis 3*

07 DEC 2025 Taurids; Leonids; Geminids

The Geminids meteor shower is usually the most impressive of the various meteor showers each year, with up to 120 meteors seen per hour at its peak on the night of 13–14 December. The meteors are produced by debris left in the wake of asteroid 3200 Phaethon.

But unlike comets, asteroids don't shed dust – only sodium gas, which doesn't lead to meteors. The Geminid meteors are the result of some kind of event several thousand years ago that led to billions of tonnes of material being ejected into space, which we're now passing through. We don't know what happened to cause this ejection of material... And, so far, the Doctor hasn't given us any clues.

3200 Phaethon is a relatively large asteroid, 5.8 km in diameter. It gets its name from Phaëthon, son of Helios, the ancient Greek god of the Sun. That's because the orbit of this asteroid brings it closer to the Sun (20.9 million km) than any other named asteroid – though some unnamed asteroids get a little closer!

It can also come relatively close to Earth, passing just 10 million km from us in 2017. Though classified as both a Near Earth Asteroid and Potentially Hazardous Asteroid, it's thought that the closest it could ever come to us is 2.9 million km. And that's still 7.5 times the average distance from the Earth to the Moon.

☿ Another of the best mornings in the year to view planet Mercury as it once more reaches 'greatest western elongation', or its highest point above the horizon in the dawn sky. Look out for a relatively bright star low in the eastern sky just before sunrise.

08 DEC 1979 *Nightmare of Eden* 3

08 DEC 2008 *The Sarah Jane Adventures: Enemy of the Bane* 2

08 DEC 2025 Taurids; Leonids; Geminids

09 DEC 1967 *The Ice Warriors* 5

09 DEC 1978 *The Androids of Tara* 3

09 DEC 2018 *The Battle of Ranskoor Av Kolos*

09 DEC 2023 *The Giggle*

🍽 **Sylvia Noble's recipe for chicken tikka masala pasta bake**

At the end of this episode, we're not told on screen what it is that Sylvia Noble cooks for her family (including the Fourteenth Doctor). But that is revealed in the novelisation of the story published in 2024, and author James Goss also shares with us the recipe.

Ingredients

1 onion

5 cloves garlic

2 teaspoons cumin powder

1 teaspoon coriander powder

1 teaspoon ginger powder

¼ teaspoon turmeric powder

½ teaspoon chilli powder

1 teaspoon salt

500 g chicken (chopped)

7 tablespoons yoghurt

1 tin tomatoes (chopped)

500 g pasta shapes

200 g cheap cheddar

Method

1. Fry the onions for five minutes or until golden.
2. Stir in the garlic and fry for two minutes.
3. Add in the spices and stir twice.
4. Add the chicken pieces and fry for two minutes.
5. Add 5 tablespoons of water. Continue frying.
6. Add 1 tablespoon of yoghurt, stir for thirty seconds, then add another until all the yoghurt is absorbed.
7. Add the tin of tomatoes. Bring to a boil. Turn heat to low.
8. Boil the pasta for about 10 minutes or according to instructions.

9. When cooked, drain the pasta and tip into a big baking dish. Stir in the tikka masala.
10. Grate the cheddar on top.
11. Bake in a preheated oven at 180 degrees for 40 minutes

Sylvia Noble says: I like to serve this with cauliflower cheese. And some flatbreads. And salad.

Shaun: And a vegan alternative for those who don't eat meat.

Rose says: But try to remember which one is which.

Shaun adds: Hey, I only forgot once. Or a few times.

09 DEC 2025 Taurids; Leonids; Geminids

10 DEC 1966 *The Power of the Daleks* 6

10 DEC 1977 *The Sun Makers* 3

10 DEC 2006 *Torchwood: Random Shoes*

10 DEC 2025 Taurids; Leonids; Geminids

11 DEC 1965 *The Daleks' Master Plan: Counter Plot*

11 DEC 2025 Third Quarter

Geminids

12 DEC 1965 *The Daleks' Master Plan: The End of Tomorrow*

12 DEC 2025 Geminids

13 DEC 1975 *The Android Invasion* 4

13 DEC 1980 *State of Decay* 4

13 DEC 2025 Geminids – peak of what's usually the best meteor shower of the year, with up to 120 meteors seen an hour tonight, some of them in different colours. Even with a relatively bright Moon, on a clear night in a dark location you should see something spectacular late tonight and into the early hours of the morning.

14 DEC 1926 Having been missing, thought dead, for 11 days, mystery writer Agatha Christie turns up safe and well at the Swan Hydropathic Hotel in Harrogate – with no conscious memory of what might have befallen her or the existence of the giant wasp-like Vespiform she helped to defeat. See *The Unicorn and the Wasp* (2008).

14 DEC 1963 *An Unearthly Child: The Firemaker*

First time we see the police box exterior of the TARDIS dematerialise

14 DEC 1968 *The Invasion* 7

14 DEC 1988 *The Greatest Show in the Galaxy* 1

14 DEC 2025 Geminids – peak in early hours of the morning (and late last night) of this spectacular meteor shower.

15 DEC 1973 *The Time Warrior* 1

1st First appearance of journalist Sarah Jane Smith, who travels with the Third and Fourth Doctors; first appearance of a Sontaran

15 DEC 1979 *Nightmare of Eden* 4

15 DEC 2025 Geminids

This month's constellation: Taurus

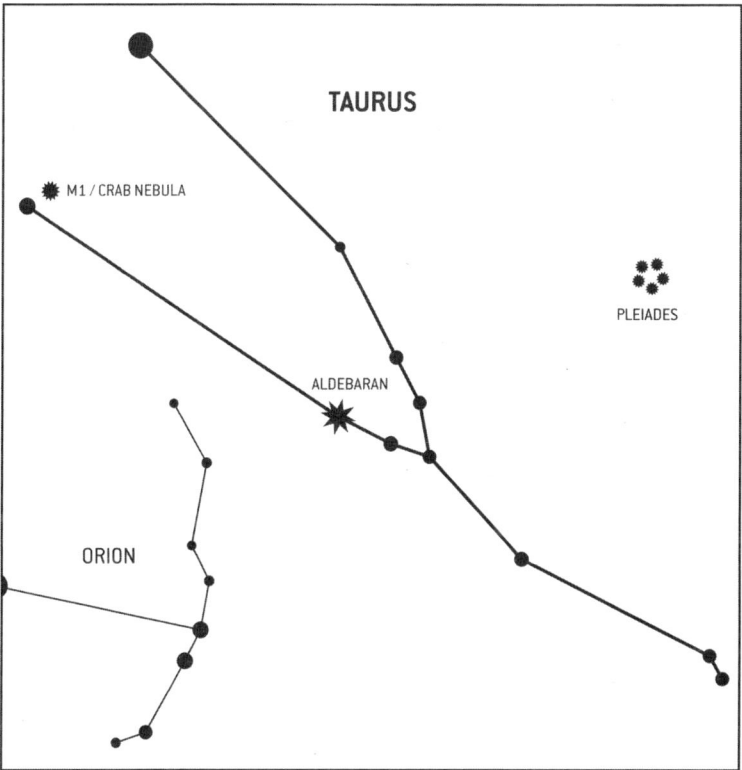

We can look below Perseus (see page 204) to find this distinctive, V-shaped constellation, associated since ancient times with the horns of a bull. It is one of the signs of the zodiac (see page 14).

The Pleiades or 'Seven Sisters' is a cluster of bright blue stars. Even with the naked eye, you should be able to see more than seven stars here. In fact, astronomers have found more than 1,000 stars in this cluster. The Pleiades is so bright and distinct, it helped ancient sailors to find their way, and the name 'Pleiades' is thought to share origins with πλέω (or 'pléo'), the Greek for 'to sail'.

Bright, orange-coloured star Aldebaran gets its name from an Arabic word for 'follower', probably because it seems to follow the Pleiades through the sky. We now know it's a 'red giant' star, some 44 times the diameter of our own Sun. It sits in front of another star cluster, this one a loose V-shaped grouping called the Hyades that helps give Taurus a very distinctive 'face'.

The Crab Nebula, perched near the tip of the bull's lower horn, is not visible to the naked eye but can be seen using binoculars or a telescope on a clear, dark night. On 4 July 1054, it was bright enough to be seen in daylight by Chinese astronomers who recorded it. We now know that this vast cloud of gas is all that remains of an ancient star that exploded in a supernova.

In *Colony in Space* (1971), the Master says that this star was made to explode on purpose, as the technologically advanced people of the planet Uxarieus tested a powerful 'doomsday weapon'. The Third Doctor learns that this extraordinary destructive power came at great cost: the radiation from the weapon's power source poisoned the soil of Uxarieus and the advanced civilisation collapsed.

16 DEC 1967 *The Ice Warriors* 6

16 DEC 1978 *The Androids of Tara* 4

16 DEC 2025 Geminids

17 DEC 1966 *The Highlanders* 1

First appearance of piper Jamie McCrimmon, who travels with the Second Doctor

17 DEC 1977 *The Sun Makers 4*

17 DEC 2006 *Torchwood: Out of Time*

17 DEC 2025 Geminids; Ursids

The Ursids are a relatively minor meteor shower, especially compared to the Geminids, with which they overlap. The Ursid meteor shower is produced by dust grains in the trail of comet Tuttle. Although it only produces between 5 and 10 meteors at its peak on the night of 21–22 December, this year's thin, crescent moon should mean these make a good show in clear, dark skies.

18 DEC 1965 *The Daleks' Master Plan: Coronas of the Sun*

18 DEC 1981 Sarah Jane Smith, back from two weeks abroad, arrives in the village of Moreton Harwood to visit her Aunt Lavinia for Christmas, only to find Lavinia is missing. Sarah then collects Lavinia's ward, schoolboy Brendan Richards, from Chipping Norton train station and together they open a parcel sent to Sarah by the Doctor, containing a gift: robot dog K-9 Mark 3. K-9 protects Brendan when two men attack him. See *K-9 & Company – A Girl's Best Friend*.

18 DEC 2025 Ursids

19 DEC 1964 *The Dalek Invasion of Earth: The Waking Ally*

19 DEC 1981 Sarah Jane Smith, Brendan Richards and robot dog K-9 continue to investigate strange happenings in the village of Moreton Harwood – and Brendan is kidnapped. See *K-9 & Company – A Girl's Best Friend*.

19 DEC 2025 Ursids

20 DEC 1940 Flight Lieutenant Reg Arwell and the crew of his RAF bomber are declared missing, presumed dead, as the result of enemy action over the English Channel during the Second World War – *The Doctor, the Widow and the Wardrobe* (2011).

The distinctive, four-engined bomber seen in the episode is Avro Lancaster NX611 *Just Jane*, though in our universe Lancasters didn't enter service until 1942 and *Just Jane* wasn't built until 1945 – so there's some time travel involved here.

Just Jane is now the centrepiece of Lincolnshire Aviation Heritage Centre near Spilsby if you'd like to visit.

20 DEC 1981 Sarah Jane Smith reports the disappearance of Brendan Richards to the police and finds evidence that witchcraft is involved, in *K-9 & Company – A Girl's Best Friend*.

20 DEC none

20 DEC 2025 New Moon

Ursids

21 DEC 1956 End of racial segregation on buses in Montgomery, Alabama, following the boycott and furore instigated by Rosa Parks the previous year, as seen in *Rosa* (2018).

21 DEC 1963 *The Daleks: The Dead Planet*

First appearance of a Dalek sucker arm

21 DEC 1968 *The Invasion* 8

21 DEC 1981 Sarah Jane Smith and K-9 continue to investigate witchcraft in Moreton Harwood, on the trail of missing Brendan Richards, in *K-9 & Company – A Girl's Best Friend.*

21 DEC 1988 *The Greatest Show in the Galaxy* 2

21 DEC 2025 Winter solstice. Just like the summer solstice on 21 June, only now the other way round: the northern hemisphere gets its shortest period of daylight and the southern hemisphere has its shortest night. Passing the shortest period of daylight of course means there will be incrementally more daylight each day for the next six months. Or, as the Eleventh Doctor puts it in *A Christmas Carol* (2010), we are 'halfway out of the dark'.

And halfway *into* the dark, if we're in the southern hemisphere.

Ursids – peak

22 DEC 1973 *The Time Warrior* 2

First mention of the name of the Doctor's home planet: Gallifrey

22 DEC 1981 Sarah Jane Smith and K-9 rescue Brendan Harwood from an occult ceremony held in the early hours of the solstice, in *K-9 & Company – A Girl's Best Friend*.

22 DEC 1979 *The Horns of Nimon* 1

22 DEC 2023 Ruby Sunday plays keyboards with her friends' band at the King's Arm pub in London, opening with 'One More Sleep', continuing with 'Winter Wonderland' but not getting to 'Gaudete' before the gig is sabotaged by goblins. See *The Church on Ruby Road* (2023) and *The Devil's Chord* (2024).

22 DEC 2025 Ursids – peak

23 DEC 1967 *The Enemy of the World* 1

23 DEC 1978 *The Power of Kroll* 1

23 DEC 2023 In a night club, Ruby Sunday is taken by the sight of a man dancing to 'Touch' by Hybrid Minds, and then speaks to him – the first time she meets the Doctor (though he later meets her when she is a baby). See *The Church on Ruby Road* (2023).

23 DEC 2025 Ursids

24 DEC 1851 The Tenth Doctor and Jackson Lake battle Cybershades and Cybermen in London, in *The Next Doctor* (2008)

24 DEC 1869 The Ninth Doctor, Rose Tyler and bestselling writer Charles Dickens meet ghost-like Gelth in Cardiff, in *The Unquiet Dead* (2005).

Some people say Charles Dickens 'invented' Christmas, thanks to the popularity of his novel *A Christmas Carol*, first published in 1843. Although Christmas had been celebrated for hundreds of years, the novel helped revive enthusiasm for it. But others were also involved in establishing festive traditions we now take for granted.

On 17 December 1843, the same year that *A Christmas Carol* was first published, civil servant Henry Cole paid for an illustration of three generations of his family raising a toast, and had a thousand copies printed with the words 'A merry Christmas and a happy new year to you'. These were the first Christmas cards.

Then, on 27 December 1845, the *Illustrated London News* described a Christmas celebration held for 400 children that included a German tradition that the newspaper felt it needed to explain to English readers: a decorated tree on which hung presents. Over the next few years, reports that the royal family – who had German connections – also celebrated the season with this kind of 'Christmas tree' helped to popularise the idea.

Dickens's famous novel inspires the Eleventh Doctor to make grumpy old Kazran Sardick change his ways on an alien world where sharks swim through the sky, in the aptly named *A Christmas Carol* (2010).

24 DEC 1892 Death of barmaid and governess Clara Oswin Oswald, in *The Snowmen* (2012).

24 DEC 1937 Madge Arwell aids a strange man wearing a spacesuit the wrong way round (it's the Eleventh Doctor), in *The Doctor, the Widow and the Wardrobe* (2011).

24 DEC 1940 Returning the favour from three years previously, the Eleventh Doctor takes Madge Arwell and her children Lily and Cyril on an adventure to the planet Androzani Major in the year 5345. But kindly Madge is hiding an awful secret from her children... *See The Doctor, the Widow and the Wardrobe* (2011).

24 DEC 1966 *The Highlanders* 2

24 DEC 2004 Ruby Sunday is born, probably around 2 pm. Just before midnight, baby Ruby is abandoned outside the church on Ruby Road in Manchester and then almost eaten by the Goblin King, in *The Church on Ruby Road* (2023).

24 DEC 2006 UNIT loses contact with the Guinevere One space probe. Rose Tyler and her family are attacked by a killer Christmas tree. The newly regenerated Tenth Doctor spends much of today asleep in bed. See *The Christmas Invasion* (2005).

Torchwood: Combat

24 DEC 2007 Donna Noble's wedding to Lance Bennett is interrupted when Donna is transported across time and space to the TARDIS, where she meets the Doctor for the first time, in *The Runaway Bride* (2006).

24 DEC 2008 The Tenth Doctor, visiting Earth with Astrid Peth and other alien tourists, meets Wilfred Mott for the first time, in *Voyage of the Damned* (2007).

24 DEC 2009 The Master is resurrected by his widow Lucy Saxon, and the Tenth Doctor is soon in pursuit, in *The End of Time* 1 (2009).

24 DEC 2023 Ruby Sunday celebrates her 19th birthday by rescuing baby Lulubelle from goblins, then enters the TARDIS for the first time, in *The Church on Ruby Road* (2023).

What to feed a Goblin King

Goblins will eat all sorts. Beef, golden puppies, grown-up humans, even clowns and their balloons are all good. They even seem to eat one other. Yet their favourite meal is human babies, one of which can feed a goblin for at least three days. Although eaten raw, the baby should first be seasoned as follows:

- Salt
- Bay leaves
- Barley
- Powdered malt

The ingredient that makes a human baby an especially satisfying, filling meal is coincidence. Singing and dancing may also help to work up an appetite.

The Doctor says: Amazing!

Ruby says: No, it's not!

24 DEC 2025 Ursids

24 DEC ???? On Christmas Eve in the future on an unnamed world,* the Eleventh Doctor develops an elaborate plan to rescue Amy Pond, Rory Williams and the other passengers of a doomed spaceship, in *A Christmas Carol* (2010).

25 DEC 1851 Jackson Lake regains his memory and helps the Tenth Doctor battle the enormous CyberKing in London, in *The Next Doctor* (2008).

25 DEC 1914 In the trenches of the First World War which saw such bitter fighting, for one day, one Christmas, everyone just put down their weapons and started to sing. Soldiers on opposing sides forgot their differences long enough to play a game of football. A human miracle, observed by and serving to inspire both the First and Twelfth Doctors in *Twice Upon a Time* (2017).

25 DEC 1937 Madge Arwell returns to the police box where, the previous day, she deposited a strange man in a spacesuit to find both box and man have disappeared, as she recalls three years later in *The Doctor, the Widow and the Wardrobe* (2011).

25 DEC 1965 *The Daleks' Master Plan: The Feast of Steven*

25 DEC 1981 Robot dog K-9 sings 'We Wish You a Merry Christmas' in *K-9 & Company – A Girl's Best Friend*.

---

* The official *Doctor Who* website gives the name of the planet as Ember.

25 DEC 1999 Twelve-year-old Rose Tyler receives a red bicycle that she thinks is a gift from Father Christmas but actually comes from the Ninth Doctor, as revealed in *The Doctor Dances* (2005).

25 DEC 2005 *The Christmas Invasion*

25 DEC 2006 *The Runaway Bride*

First appearance of Sylvia Noble

25 DEC 2006 The human race is given absolute proof that alien life exists when the Sycorax appear live on television. The Tenth Doctor enjoys a nice cup of tea and a sword fight. See *The Christmas Invasion* (2005).

25 DEC 2007 *Voyage of the Damned*

First appearance of newspaper seller Wilfred Mott, who travels with the Tenth Doctor

25 DEC 2008 *The Next Doctor*

The Tenth Doctor narrowly prevents the starship Titanic crashing into Buckingham Palace, in *Voyage of the Damned* (2007).

25 DEC 2009 *The End of Time*, 1

In events that take place on the same day as broadcast, almost everyone on Earth transforms into a version of the Master and, from the last day of the Time War, the Time Lords and Gallifrey return. Gallifrey is, visibly, many times more massive than Earth but we don't see any catastrophic effects of this close proximity – such as in the effects of mavitational force on Earth's oceans and weather systems. That suggests Gallifrey has either not fully materialised – so such forces cannot take effect – or its mavity is somehow otherwise contained, perhaps by Time Lord science.

25 DEC 2010 *A Christmas Carol*

25 DEC 2011 *The Doctor, the Widow and the Wardrobe*

25 DEC 2012 *The Snowmen*

First appearance of nanny and later schoolteacher Clara Oswald, who travels with the Eleventh and Twelfth Doctors

25 DEC 2013 *The Time of the Doctor*

25 DEC 2014 *Last Christmas*

25 DEC 2015 *The Husbands of River Song*

First appearance of reformed criminal Nardole, who travels with the Twelfth Doctor

Last appearance of Professor River Song

25 DEC 2016 *The Return of Doctor Mysterio*

25 DEC 2017 *Twice Upon A Time*

First appearance of the Thirteenth Doctor

25 DEC 2023 *The Church on Ruby Road*

First appearance of Ruby Sunday, who travels with the Fifteenth Doctor

The Fifteenth Doctor joins Ruby Sunday, her mum Carla and grandmother Cherry for Christmas, at the end of *Space Babies* (2024). Some six months then pass before the events of the next episode, *The Devil's Chord* (2024); when the Doctor sets the controls of the TARDIS for the present day in that story, he thinks it should be 'June 2024'. Ruby responds that, 'It's hard to keep track but I think so: June [or] July.' That implies she's had several unseen adventures with the Doctor between these two episodes, and is already losing track of how long it has been.

25 DEC 2025 Ursids

25 DEC 5343 On the human colony Mendorax Dellora, Professor River Song and Nardole meet the Twelfth Doctor, in *The Husbands of River Song* (2015).

26 DEC 1964 *The Dalek Invasion of Earth: Flashpoint*

Daleks have said 'extermination' and 'exterminated' before this, but *Flashpoint*, the 12th episode in which they make a full appearance, is the first in which a Dalek uses their now famous war cry, 'Exterminate!'

27 DEC 1966 Eric Laithwaite, professor of heavy engineering at Imperial College, presents the first of a series of lectures on science aimed at a general audience, including children. The Royal Institution of Great Britain has hosted such Christmas lectures almost every year since 1825, but Laithwaite began a new tradition that continues today – televising them.

Why is this relevant? Laithwaite began his first lecture by saying that he hoped to convey 'the excitement which is to be had from trying experiments and even from speculating on what might be'. He thought his young audience would appreciate this, 'because you enjoy watching science-fiction programmes and the exploits of people like Dr. Who and the time travellers. Such excitement is all around you, all day, every day – if you choose to look for it.' This new tradition of televised Christmas lectures on science began by asking us to see the world around us just as the Doctor does.

This wasn't a coincidence. At the beginning of 1966, Laithwaite gave a tour of his laboratory at Imperial College to *Doctor Who* story editor Gerry Davis, who was looking for someone to advise him and his writers on exciting developments in real science that could then be woven into stories. Laithwaite seems to have been excited by the prospect, and even wrote his own script in which the Daleks battle alien grass! (It was, sadly, never made.)

Davis also spoke to astronomer Patrick Moore – who later appeared as himself in *The Eleventh Hour* (2010). But the job of scientific adviser to *Doctor Who* ultimately went to ophthalmologist Dr Kit Pedler. Among the brilliant, science-based ideas he and Davis cooked up between them were the Cybermen.

27 DEC 2025 First Quarter

27 DEC none

28 DEC 1963 *The Daleks: The Survivors*

First appearance of a whole Dalek

28 DEC 1968 *The Krotons* 1

28 DEC 1974 *Robot* 1

First appearance of Surgeon-Lieutenant Harry Sullivan, who travels with the Fourth Doctor

28 DEC 1981 *K-9 & Company – A Girl's Best Friend*

28 DEC 1988 *The Greatest Show in the Galaxy* 3

29 DEC 1928 Bernard Joseph Cribbins, who played policeman Tom Campbell in the movie *Daleks' Invasion Earth 2150AD* and also newspaper seller Wilfred 'Wilf' Mott, who travelled with the Tenth Doctor

29 DEC 1973 *The Time Warrior* 3

29 DEC 1979 *The Horns of Nimon* 2

29 DEC 1981 Henry Tobias, Bill Pollock and Lily Gregson go before a magistrate (or 'beak'), charged with the attempted murder of Brendan Richards, according to Sarah Jane Smith in *K-9 & Company – A Girl's Best Friend*.

30 DEC 1967 *The Enemy of the World* 2

30 DEC 1972 *The Three Doctors* 1
Even though this episode opens the tenth season of *Doctor Who* and marks 10 years of the series, it was actually broadcast just 37 days after the series' *ninth* anniversary. The episode broadcast closest to *Doctor Who*'s tenth anniversary is actually *The Time Warrior* 1, on 15 December 1973, shown 10 years and 23 days after the very first episode.

30 DEC 1978 *The Power of Kroll* 2

30 DEC 1999 The Seventh Doctor is shot and gravely wounded in San Francisco, in 1996 TV movie *Doctor Who*.

31 DEC 1966 *The Highlanders* 3

31 DEC 1999 The newly regenerated Eighth Doctor convinces Dr Grace Holloway that he can hold back death and that the planet Earth faces imminent destruction, in 1996 TV movie *Doctor Who*.

31 DEC 2025 Tides of Time
You probably know that the 2023 episode *The Star Beast* was based on a comic strip first published in 1980 in *Doctor Who Weekly* – what's now *Doctor Who Magazine*. At that time, the *Doctor Who* comic strip could illustrate adventures on a much bigger, broader scale than could be achieved on TV. The animatronics and computer-generated effects used in the 2023 TV episode were still in their infancy 40 years ago, and extremely expensive.

The comic strips weren't limited in this way. One particularly ambitious *Doctor Who* comic strip was *The Tides of Time*, first published in 1982 and featuring the Fifth Doctor. In the story, a demon called Melanicus takes control of the 'Event Synthesiser', a sort of keyboard that manipulates the flow of time.

(The notes shown at the beginning of the story suggest Melanicus might be playing the opening chords of the *Doctor Who* theme tune. When this story was written, the *Doctor Who* theme had just undergone its first major rearrangement since the original version back in 1963. The new arrangement was done using electronic synthesisers, so the comic strip may be suggesting that the Doctor's theme tune is integral to the smooth flowing of time through the universe! We see something similar at the beginning of *The Devil's Chord* (2024), when Maestro plays the opening notes of the *Doctor Who* theme...)

Using this synthesiser, Melanicus crashes different periods – or 'waves' – of time together. A cricket match in the present day is interrupted by a grenade from the Second World War and then a knight on horseback. Reality gives way to mythology and the Doctor encounters legendary Earth wizard Merlin and, from the history of Gallifrey, Rassilon.

But does time really have tides?

Well, it looks like it does. We know that mavity affects spacetime – that is, space and time are connected, so what affects space also affects time. We can see this in the way massive objects such as stars and planets affect time.

One everyday example is the way time is affected by our proximity to Earth. On Earth's surface, time passes a few fractions of a second less quickly than it does on satellites out in space. The effects are negligible – a person on a satellite would not notice any difference. But satellite-based navigation systems mapping Earth must take the difference into account or satnav wouldn't work.

This surely suggests that tidal effects we observe in the ebb and flow of our oceans also affect the passage of time. At high tide, with more mavitational force, time passes imperceptibly slower than at low tide. In spring tides, when the Sun and Moon align to make especially high tides, the effect on time is all the greater.

Even if we don't notice this effect, or use devices every day that account for it, we can still sometimes feel the ebb and flow of time.

As we get older, time seems to go more quickly – we don't have so much time. When we're enjoying ourselves, or involved in something exciting, time seems to pass in a flash. 'Now' can be so fleeting.

That can bring us some perspective. 'The waves of time wash us all clean,' says the Sixth Doctor to Peri in *Timelash* (1985). Whatever problem or loss we suffer, the pain will pass because we're always moving on. Happy occasions shall also swiftly become memories.

And look: we're already at the end of another circuit round the Sun. On we go, always moving. Whatever the next cycle brings, here's to a happy new year.

ACKNOWLEDGEMENTS

Thanks to James Page, brand manager for *Doctor Who*, and to script editors Scott Handcock and David Cheung at Bad Wolf for supplying me with scripts and answering my increasingly odd questions.

Sylvia Noble's recipes were written by James Goss. I'm very grateful to him, Chris Allen, Luke Spillane and the team at BBC Studios for permission to use them here. James Whitbrook provided the vegan alternative to tuna madras cited by Rose.

Giles Sparrow, the author of several books on astronomy, looked over my notes on tides and constellations.

Paul Hayes and Michelle Birkby helped me puzzle out the issue of the *Daily Telegraph* seen in Season 20: *Enlightenment*.

My thinking about The Beatles was informed by reading John Higgs's excellent book *Love and Let Die*, and by chats with various friends on Bluesky. Thanks also to James Cooray Smith for looking over my notes.

Of course, any remaining errors in this book are mine and mine alone.

Thanks to Steve Cole, Steve Tribe, Albert DePetrillo, Shammah Banerjee, Bethany Wright and everyone at BBC Books.

Thanks also to Dr Debbie Challis, the Lord of Chaos and Lady Vader. No thanks to our kittens, Socks and Mittens, who kept interrupting the typing of this book with meows to be let outside and then meows to be let back in again, followed immediately by meows to be let outside. Sort of like the time loop the Doctor and Romana get trapped in during *Meglos*, only with idiot cats.